MARCELO

BOOK ONE OF THE MENDACITY SERIES

AYRLEAH TULL

This is a work of fiction. Names, characters, places, and incidents either are the product of the author's imagination or are used fictitiously. Any resemblance to actual persons, living or dead, events, or locales is entirely coincidental.

Copyright © 2020 by Ayrleah Tull

All rights reserved. No part of this book may be reproduced or used in any manner without written permission of the copyright owner except for the use of quotations in a book review. For more information, address: Ayrleah.tull123@gmail.com

First paperback edition December 2020

Cover designed by tjmbookcovers.com

Image © Depositphotos

ISBN 9780645053609 (paperback)

ISBN 9780645053616 (ebook)

❦ Created with Vellum

For Gab

CHAPTER 1

THREE YEARS PRIOR

"Yes Roux, you may be completely lost but it's totally not your fault," I reasoned. I mean was I going to die? Okay, possibly. Was it enough to make me rethink my decision? No. Day one of being the new girl in the big city and I had already managed to get myself in a bind. At this rate, I had no reason to even be nervous for tomorrow, it seemed I wasn't going to make it back to my dorm, let alone to my first day of university. Not when the shadows crawled closer, the further I ran down the alleyway, subtly reminding me that nothing good ever came from getting up early.

This morning had been different though. I knew I needed to distract myself, laying around all day in my new dorm was not going to ease my nerves. As my stomach twisted, eyes darting over the dim backroad, I wasn't too sure if my dose of morning air was helping. I just hoped that it was cold enough for me to develop the flu before tomorrow, that way I wouldn't need to worry about my classes for at least another week.

The backstreets of the city were far from pleasant,

however, they made up for their unkempt appearance with solidarity, which was definitely a bonus when it came to me and exercising. The path that my phone mapped out for me before I left the campus this morning, abruptly stopped. My feet tangled in a mess that nearly had me throwing myself at the floor. The orange cones and yellow fences had my lips rolling in to hold back a groan. Absolutely fantastic, I thought, roadworks. I eyed the unfamiliar path to my left with distaste, the bags of trash piled high onto the big green dumpsters were not appealing in the slightest. Of course, unless I wanted to turn around and walk all the way back to the main street that I had turned off, it would have to do. Surely it would lead roughly in the same direction.

My headphones tangled in my hands as I began fiddling with them, strolling down the murky alley. The stench from the bags of what had to be rotten food and dirty clothes made me gag as I quickly jogged past. The traffic may not have been terrible this far from the city centre, however the echoes carried far past the outskirts of town and left me on edge.

The beat of the music had me pushing my legs in a rhythm that carried me further from the street lights, away from the skyline view. If it were any other morning, I was sure I would have been put off, the darkness swallowing me in one sudden snap of its jaws, as I flung myself around the corner. Of course, I had bigger things to worry about compared to the uncertainty the alley held, like what tomorrow would bring. A whole new beginning, a bunch of random strangers and probably the most stressful classes of my life. With all this mixed together, I could only imagine how terrible it was going to be.

The shadows clambered closer to me, the deeper into the maze I strode. One lonely apartment had a light flickering above as I passed, as if peering down at me.

A loud clang sounded suddenly in the alley. Oh my gosh, I thought. Way to go Roux, now you're lost and scared. My muscles had tensed, skin rolling with goosebumps that travelled up my spine. My feet skidded to an abrupt stop as I ripped my earphones out. Silence. There was no movement within the darkness, the distant city the only sound reverberating throughout the alley. Shivering, I peered around the small patch of path that wasn't obscured by the darkness. I was sure I had heard something. Yet other than the scraps of rubbish scattered along the edges of the path, there seemed to be nothing there. Just darkness. Good grief, I thought. Now I was going crazy.

I willed my feet to move forward out of the small space. I needed to find a way to circle back into the busy streets. The faster I got to the city, the quicker I could relax back into the hustle of people and start setting up my new dorm. I really should have done it when I had arrived, but the churning of my stomach at the unfamiliarity of it all had made me think unclearly. Hence, why I had decided to try and calm myself with the most dreadful thing on the planet... Exercise. I would never have done such a thing in my usual state of mind. My stiff knees clenched as I took a few steps forward. The eerie silence still taunted me.

My breath drew in quickly. Come on Roux, you're being an idiot. I rolled my shoulders and started walking again, pocketing the headphones. The alley, thick with the tension rolling off from me, seemed almost claustrophobic now. Tall brick buildings peering down at me, caving me in. The hair on my arms stood straight, the bumps gripped my arms tightly.

I jumped. Something beside me had moved. Scampering against the wall on the other side of the alley, I couldn't seem to draw a breath as the air from my lungs rushed out. My pulse quickened, dread filling me. I tried to draw in a breath, my lungs screaming as I stared into the pits of darkness. Somewhere, a shadow dashed and I found my mind unable to communicate with my muscles. Leave. I needed to get out of here.

It seemed to pick up speed, the mass moving forward faster. My chest contracted in fright, muscles unmoving as I tried to scream. It lunged, my body almost collapsed down the wall in fear. I squealed as it landed only a foot away. My eyes had widened, pulse pumping loudly and muscles spasming. Oh my gosh. A cat. I sucked in a quick breath, tears stinging my eyes as my quiet sobs turned to fearful laughter. It was just a cat. I was an idiot. It peered up at me curiously, its yellow eyes pouring into my own. Its sleek coat and thin body glimmered in the low light, before the black creature slunk away, back into its shadowy den.

Giggling at myself, I pushed off the wall, my feet scraping against the rubble on the floor as I drew in a steady breath. Just a cat. I had taken a single step when I heard it again. Clanging. Grunting. Someone was here. They were close. I held my breath as I peered into the darkness. My body willing me to continue standing in silence, whilst my mind screamed to run. I threw myself into the shadows of the walls as something moved quickly ahead. It was not a cat.

I held my breath. My head quickly grew dizzy. Don't move-don't make a sound, I chanted in my mind. I had no idea what to do as the shadows continued to move. No idea where to go. My breathing quickened as the grunts grew louder, I could tell they were men, their muddled angry screams causing me to wobble on my feet.

"I should have known," someone grunted.

Although their words could hardly be heard over the sound of thuds and slaps, the gravelly voice of the man still had my pulse quickening.

"You're a traitor! A liar! Just wait until *he* finds out!"

MARCELO

A thud had me biting my cheek to stop from screaming, the yelp that followed causing me to almost draw blood.

Oh my gosh. I needed to get out of here.

I clutched myself tighter as a male voice rang throughout the space in a tangled scream of rage. My breathing caught again as I pressed closer to the wall.

"*He* will never know! Because you aren't gonna say shit!"

I could feel my pulse throbbing throughout my body. If I left the shadows of the alleyway, I was sure to be seen, if I stayed I was closer to getting caught.

My chest roared at me to breathe and my muscles cramped from tensing. I had no idea what to do. The noises grew closer. My breathing quickened as I slid down the wall. I needed to make myself smaller. My lips wobbled, hands clutched over my head, my knees hiding my face. I clenched as the yelling grew louder.

BANG!

My body forced me to shoot up, the distinctive sound of a gunshot ripping through the alley had me running blindly. I took it back, this was enough to make me rethink escaping the university! I needed to get away. Someone was screaming. Footsteps seemed to pound along the cold floor before disappearing quickly. Tears ran down my cheeks, the cold wind freezing them on my face. Oh my gosh. I wanted to wail. I wanted to scream! This wasn't fair! I had only been here one day! I couldn't die! I hadn't been anywhere or accomplished anything!

I had to get out of the backstreets. My mind couldn't comprehend which way to go. Crack! Another gunshot. A shriek. My legs wobbled faster, propelling me towards the rising sunlight. I was almost at the end of the alleyway, the light leaking around the corner.

"Help," a small, choked voice whimpered.

Spinning before I could stop myself, I saw him. Crawling

from the shadows of the alley like a contortionist, his body morphed with pain. My breath hitched, heart pounding.

He looked as shocked as I felt, peering up at me with wide green eyes. Shuffling backwards, clutching his side. His wide eyes held mine in a tight grip. I took a step back, his ragged breath, a desperate whisper that filled the alley with tension.

"Please."

I halted. My feet ached to keep moving. My mind begging me to run. The large, tattooed stranger, struggled to prop himself up on the brick wall, a strangled cry coming from his mouth. I took another step away at the sight of blood flowing quickly over his hand. My stomach churned and I swallowed. His shirt was red. Bright red. Hands cradled the side of his chest, where blood started to pool underneath him.

For a second, my whole body screamed at me to move. No one would know I was here. I could get to safety easily. I was so close to the corner.

His eyes flew to mine again in a desperate plea and I knew my choice had already been made. Sprinting, landing at his feet in a heap of sobs, I ripped my phone out and dialled. It only rang twice but those two rings felt like an eternity.

"Emergency services, what is your emergency?"

"Hi," I rushed, hitting the speaker button. "There's a man," I looked him over, a sob escaping. "He's injured, he's been shot, I don't know what to do, we're in one of the backstreets of the city, the north side!"

"Calm down please ma'am, what street exactly, are there any street signs around you? A building name maybe, anything you can see?"

No, I thought as I frantically looked around. There was nothing.

"The alley off Park Street," the man grunted up at me.

"An alley off Park Street," I repeated unsurely.

There was a short pause and my stomach flipped.

"Don't worry, ma'am, help is on the way, can you tell me what the wound looks like, is the person conscious?"

"Yes, he's conscious, there's lots of blood, it's everywhere," I sobbed, unable to see anything through the mass of crimson.

"Okay ma'am stay calm, Im going to need you to apply pressure to the wound. Can you do that for me?"

I nodded, cursing briefly at myself as I realised how stupid I was.

"Yes."

The rest became a blur of pure instinct. His blood stained me as I pressed my hands to his side. The sticky substance continued to weep out over the alley floor, the metallic smell watering my mouth with the urge to vomit. I had never witnessed someone in so much pain before. His constant grunts as he shook with sobs had me pressing my hands harder, hoping to slow the bleeding.

He stilled, a brief moment of dread washed over me, before a loud groan echoed through the alley. I could only hope I was right in applying pressure. My cries matched his as the blood continued to run over my fingers, flowing to the ground. My eyes snapped shut. I didn't have the guts to watch someone die.

"I, I don't know how to do this," I whispered, hoping that the lady on the phone didn't hear me and that the man understood that I was speaking to him. My hands shook from the pressure on his wound.

When I finally worked up the courage to open my eyes, his green ones met mine and for a brief moment, my world stopped spinning. I thought he was gone, his eyes unmoving, staring into my own. A chuckling cough shook his body, and I found myself sighing in relief, before he groaned again.

"You're doing great," his voice was rough, a pant as he

forced a smile up at me, it quickly contorted back into a grimace.

I jumped, his hand settled to rest on top of mine, pushing harder into his skin. I wasn't sure how much longer he had. I didn't know how much blood someone could lose before they died, however, looking into the alley, I was sure it couldn't be much more.

I had no idea what to say. No idea how to comfort such a man in such a state.

"You really shouldn't be too stressed," he ground out, squeezing his eyes shut, pain evident on his face. "I probably deserved it."

I watched him completely bewildered, a single breath of laughter falling from his lips, as if he found what he said funny. I didn't. No one deserved this.

"I should have known it was a set up," he continued, trying to hold back his chuckles as he grimaced. "Fucking idiot."

"What's your name?" I asked, hoping to distract him as I peered down at him. If he was going to die in my arms, it was the least I needed.

"Declan," he whispered as he began to slowly relax into my arms, his eyes unfoccusing to look at the sky. Oh no. Oh gosh, this couldn't be fucking happening. I wasn't ready. He looked at me again, seeming to realise my stress.

"Yours?" He bit out, smiling up at me.

I sighed at his movements, before I opened my mouth, then snapped it shut. Paramedics and police officers spewed into the alley, some with guns, others pulling a stretcher and various other items.

An officer ran quickly ahead, gripping Declan's face tightly, concern spreading over him before he was pulled back by the medical team. They didn't hesitate as Declan groaned in pain, lifting him onto the stretcher. Masks and an assortment of tubes were pulled from various bags and I had no idea what to do as I stood watching pathetically, wringing my hands in anxiety as he was quickly wheeled away.

His hand dangled over the edge, seeming lifeless. I rushed to grab it, prop it back on the stretcher. I needed to go with him. To make sure he was alright.

However, I couldn't take a single step, the police officer jumped in my way and held a hand out to stop me. He seemed in pain as he looked between Declan and myself, almost as if he wanted to follow him.

"We need a statement," he ground out, pushing me to the other officers.

My lungs constricted in on themselves, my chest tight as I peered over my shoulder at the stretcher being wheeled around the corner, out of sight. My mind buzzed with the images of him as my sobs turned to hiccups and I heard the sound of sirens, fading as the ambulance drove away.

CHAPTER 2

PRESENT DAY

Zach slept peacefully beside me. Early morning sunlight streamed calmly over his features. I scowled, the warm rays brought me no relaxation in the early hours. It was a well-known fact that I, Roux Fallon, was not a morning person. So the fact that I was up at this hour, whining over the thought that someone so smart couldn't figure out how to please a woman was honestly just sad. Not that I could ever tell him this, we both knew we weren't anything other than friends. If you could even call us that. The thought of having to have *that* type of conversation with Zach, the meaningful kind, made my skin crawl with nerves. It wasn't that I was nervous of what he would say or do. I didn't particularly care about any of that. I just didn't want him to think that my concerns equalled feelings because the last thing I needed right now was for him to think we were going to be anything else other than just friends.

What made matters worse, was that on mornings like these, he liked to linger. Like a bad smell, or a bug. It was annoying enough to make me want to bang my head against the headboard. I knew I shouldn't have let him in last night.

Not when I had an eight AM lecture this morning. I should have continued the night studying. However, studying made me frustrated and frustration led to no self-control. Especially around a perplexity such as Zach, who had arrived unexpectedly and was ready to make all my worries drift away. I couldn't turn down an opportunity to let off some steam.

But, it hadn't seemed to work. It took him ten minutes to do his business, before he settled down into my bed ready to spoon. I huffed, pouting at how my morning was turning out. It was official. I had sadly, overused Zach. Grown accustomed to him, there was no longer any room for excitement. However, he obviously wasn't used to me, not with what he had shown last night, having left me utterly disappointed yet again.

Frowning, I tapped my phone. 7:20. I had forty minutes to shower, get dressed and get to class. Great. This was exactly what I wanted to avoid in university. Distractions. All I needed was to finish this year, get my English degree and then I'd be free.

My eyes rolled as I shuffled awkwardly underneath Zach's heavy arm, his eyes fluttering. A flicker of hope passed through me.

"Good morning," I whispered forcefully, trying to prompt him to stay awake. A slow smile spread over his face and I silently cheered at my victory. Pulling me in closer, he sighed. I held back the urge to groan.

"Well it is a good morning if you're here," he mumbled.

Resisting an eye-roll at his poor efforts, and holding back a gag towards the smell of cheap alcohol on his breath, I wiggled in his arms.

"I have to shower," I stated, hoping he would understand I was in a rush.

He sighed, pouting his thin lips, before slowly releasing me, rolling onto his back.

"I could join"

"No," I rushed, cutting him off. I needed as much space between us as possible so that I could focus on getting ready and walking to class on time. Perhaps Quinn and I could even get a coffee on the way if I hurried.

He looked at me sadly for a moment before a smirk made its way to his lips.

"You're right," he grinned. "You might be a little late for your lecture with what I had planned."

I highly doubted that.

I laughed half-heartedly as I jumped out of bed, Zach's eyes following me to my dresser. I collected my clothes, trying not to make it seem as though I was put off by his stares. He sat, silently watching me, arms folded behind his head in an obvious attempt to show his muscles. I rolled my eyes, it would have been attractive if he hadn't tried to flaunt it.

I was glad the old dorm rooms on campus at least had an ensuite. There wasn't much else to them, unless you paid for the newly renovated blocks. However, I was grateful, it beat having to walk to a communal bathroom. As I walked in, I made sure to lock the door before I stripped. I wasn't risking Zach trying to sneak in and have some 'fun'. I didn't want to seem overly rude. I seriously just didn't have time. At least not for mediocrity.

The shower, which barely held my soap, let alone my body, slowly heated, while I stood shivering and waiting for it to warm-up. Come on. Come on. As the water started streaming warm, I jumped under, scrubbing quickly. A brief thought of how I really should have washed my hair fluttered, before I swatted it away. I didn't have time.

My skin burned as I rinsed and turned the tap off,

however as I jumped out, I couldn't have cared less. My usual skin was pink as my tights and turtleneck were thrown on in a rush. My auburn hair pulled back in a low bun. At least this way no one could see the greasiness. Good job Roux, I snickered at myself.

Walking out I noticed Zach still sat on my bed, looking at his phone.

I walked over, grabbing my own, checking the time. Oh gosh. 7:40. Oh gosh. I really needed to go if I was going to walk to the lecture hall.

"I uh,"

"I know, you gotta go," he said, as he ripped the blankets off, thankfully in his boxers.

"Yeah." Like now, especially if I was going to meet Quinn. This was the one class we shared.

He slipped into his tight blue jeans quickly, throwing his shirt over his head as he turned.

"I had fun last night, Roux," he smiled.

I forced a smile back.

"Me too."

As he opened the door, he stopped abruptly, almost ramming into a frazzled Quinn. She looked shocked to see him standing there and yet, not surprised.

"Quinn," Zach mumbled walking out.

I caught Quinn's eye-roll, as she walked around him.

"Zach."

She wasted no time in shutting the door, turning to look at me with her arms crossed. I tried to ignore her, grabbing my keys and papers.

"You can't keep stringing that guy along," she said, shaking her head.

I raised an eyebrow.

"Okay mum."

"Roux," she groaned, cutting me off.

I frowned.

"Zach knows very well that this is just physical," I stated. It was true. We had both agreed at the beginning that we didn't want a relationship.

"It doesn't mean he still agrees with that," she frowned.

I didn't get what her point was. I wasn't doing anything wrong here. We had an agreement.

Ignoring her, I picked up my book bag. She flopped down on my bed, arms spread wide as she sighed. I looked at her in shock. Her eyes met mine, confusion crossing her features before realisation and she sprung up as if the bed had caught fire.

"I should not have done that," she said, staring at the bed in disdain. I laughed.

"No, you shouldn't have," I teased. I needed to wash my sheets when I got back.

I picked up my jacket, eyeing her as she checked her watch.

"I'm ready," I grinned, understanding her eagerness to leave.

She rolled her eyes, taking my arm in hers.

"I didn't say anything," she mumbled.

I shook my head and laughed at her sheepish smile.

"As for Zach," I said. "He doesn't need to agree that we should keep it just physical. If he has a problem with being just friends he can bring it up himself."

Her big brown eyes rolled dramatically.

"Besides, he didn't seem to have an issue with it last night."

She smirked, pulling me out of the dorms and onto the path that led us to the lecture halls.

"Was it better than last time?" she asked, knowing very well how disappointing it had been lately.

I must have given her a sarcastic look, as she broke out in

laughter, drawing the attention of a few students around us. I tried to shush her, looking away.

"That bad huh?" She laughed.

I rolled my eyes, blushing.

"You have no idea."

CHAPTER 3

I laughed at Quinn, grumbling from across the other side of the booth.

"I just don't get it," she moped.

Caspers was full of students ready for their coffee fix. I didn't blame them. Caspers had to be the best cafe in the city, and we were graced with its presence on campus. Thank goodness. I needed a decent coffee after that migraine of a lecture.

"Don't get what?" I laughed. Quinn had a tendency to be dramatic, her eyes rolling into the back of her head as she groaned, bringing her cup of hot chocolate to her mouth, taking a gulp.

"I don't get," she started. "How, in a whole campus of males, I can't seem to find one who's desperate enough to date me!"

I rolled my eyes. Quinn was stunning, she and I both knew that every guy wanted her. I knew however, that the issue wasn't the male population themselves but instead that she wanted a specific one.

"How is William?" I asked. I smirked as her cheeks grew hot with a flush.

"This isn't about Will," she grumbled.

We both knew it was.

"Please." I laughed. "I just don't get why you haven't asked him out yet." I smirked. Quinn rolled her eyes.

Yes I did. William Thox, son of the university chairman, absolutely gorgeous, friends with Quinn since diapers and completely oblivious to her infatuation. Although, I was sure if she spoke up, there wouldn't be a single doubt in his mind about how he felt. It was obvious that the two were just too blind to see that they had the perfect thing going on.

"He's my best friend Quinn."

"Hey!" I pouted, offended. "I'm your best friend."

"You know what I mean!" She laughed, throwing herself back in her seat dramatically. "He's just-just,"

"Perfect," I cut her off, rolling my eyes. I had heard this speech many times.

"But he is," she whined. "And I'm just me," she finished with a huff, lifting her cup to her lips.

"Quinn, you're the most overly-dramatic, oblivious person that I've ever met."

Her mouth dropped open at my words.

"But you're also the best person I know. You're beautiful and you are going to graduate top of your acting class. Not to mention that you're a shoe in for the dramatic arts internship. If he can't see how amazing you are, he doesn't deserve you."

She looked at me thoughtful for a moment, before a smile appeared on her face.

"You're right."

I nodded. *Yes I was.*

I winced mid-sip of my coffee, as I realised it had gone cold. If there was a list of everything I disliked, it would probably be extremely long, but the first three things would be cold coffee. The fourth would be anyone using my full name. I shuddered at the thought.

"If any of us should be talking about our guy problems though…"

I gave her the most deadpan look I could muster.

"Okay, okay," she grumbled. I swear, if anyone heard us speak they'd think we hated each other. I blamed it on our personalities, we were too much alike for our own good.

"Wanna head to the gym in the morning?" she asked.

The gym. I retract my earlier statement. Number two on my list would be exercise. It never led to anything good.

"Nah, I have a study session in the library."

"You study too much," she frowned.

"Not all of us are wildly talented."

Her laughter filled the cafe, most men's necks craning to look over at her. I didn't blame them. Even the way she laughed was pretty.

"Oh shut up Roux, you're top of your class!"

Yes, because I study, I thought.

My croissant flaked over the table as I picked at it. It was growing later into the evening, most customers had come and gone while we sat and spoke. The only other students sat a few tables back, crowded with athletically dressed boys. If I was going to get up early enough to be at the study session before six, I would have to start getting ready to head home and cook something.

"Want to come to mine for dinner?" I asked.

Quinn laughed as she crumbled her croissant wrapper.

"You mean all the way from our kitchen?" she gasped sarcastically.

The communal kitchen on our floor wasn't terrible, but I would rather watch a movie on my laptop than mingle with the new freshmen on our floor. If only they knew what was to come, they wouldn't seem so preppy. It's all fun and games in the first year, filled with savings and no one to frown upon your choices. Now that I was in my last year, I could only look back and squint disappointedly at myself. Just as I could squint disapprovingly at the preppy freshmen. However, Quinn had told me not to be rude and her dorm was a mess.

"What are we having?" she asked as we packed up our table.

The last half of Quinn's croissant, that she had been saving, fell to the floor. Her mouth dropped open and I couldn't help but snicker. Quinn did love her food. She bent down to pick it up, pouting as our eyes met and we burst out in laughter.

"I can make us pasta?" I offered.

She bit her lip and shrugged.

"I have some chicken that needs cooking…"

"Sweet."

Things were really starting to look up.

I smiled as the door swung open, cold air hit my face. My eyes stung in the winter weather. I was determined to make my last year on campus, one of greatness.

CHAPTER 4

This was the worst plan I had ever agreed to. I argued with myself, that perhaps a few more hours of studying, no matter the hour of day, would be beneficial. I wasn't sure who I had been trying to fool. Roux Fallon and early mornings went together about as well as ice cream and tomato sauce. Especially when it was a Saturday, meaning Casper's would be closed and I would have to sit through a gruelling study session at five thirty in the morning without a caffeine hit. I pitied the poor souls that waited for me in the library. This morning had ensured that today was going to be terrible.

Usually we would have studied in the west side library. However, the study rooms had already been taken. So now, toes freezing and muscles stiff from the cold morning air, I had to walk half an hour across campus to the east side. Fortunately, the east side had recently been renovated, ensuring that the heating was bound to be much better than I was used to.

I grimaced as the cold wind slapped across my face. Winter

was definitely not my favourite season, though the thought of the nearing spring brought comfort. In a few more months I would be out of here and hopefully proving that something good could come from an English degree. I had set myself up from the moment I stepped foot on campus, making sure I attended almost every class, turning down opportunities for interference. I built my own bridge to success and nothing could get in my way. Unless, of course, I didn't graduate top of my class. That would surely put a bump in the road. I doubted Briggs Publishing looked for mediocre candidates in their summer writing program. I had put in the effort though, I made sure of it, I needed this as much as a poet needed inspiration and I wouldn't allow myself to fail. Writing was my dream, my passion, and I wouldn't let myself down.

My phone tickled my leg, as it buzzed in my pocket.

'Susie's sick, study group cancelled, back to norm next week- Han.'

Susie's sick, sick my butt! Susie's still curled up in bed, not wanting to walk in the freezing cold more like it! To think! I had gotten up early! I mean, at five o'clock in the morning! For this! My foot made contact with a small pile of half melted snow, clumps flying as I kicked it. I wanted to send back that they could all shove it somewhere dark. I didn't though. Hannah had been nice enough to invite me along this week, I couldn't be rude now.

"*No problem,*" I replied.

Huffing, I looked back towards the tall dorm building on the west side. It was almost a fifteen minute walk back, or a twenty minute walk to the city, where I could only hope some form of a café would be open and willing to serve an extra strong coffee. If I was up this early, it may as well have been for a good reason. I couldn't think of anything better to fill the tired void than caffeine.

Pouting, I eyed Caspers ahead. *If only you were open*, I thought, as I watched the familiar double doors in disdain.

I began walking half-heartedly, past the cafe and to the city centre. I could always message Quinn, she wouldn't be up quite this early, however, soon enough her alarm would be blaring, desperately trying to pull her from her sleep to convince her to head to the gym. I shuddered at the thought of her morning routine. Getting up early and going to the gym...for fun? The thought of having to do push-ups or burpees or whatever it was that she did, sounded like torture. At least I was now braving the cold for something meaningful...coffee.

I tensed as something moved within the shadows up ahead, but rolled my eyes at my nerves. I wasn't in some abandoned alley, I was in the middle of campus, there was no need to feel scared.

The sun had even started to come up, peeking over the sky rise buildings in the distance. I sighed in relief. Nothing bad happened in the daylight, not like it did in the darkness. Still, my muscles remained tense as the breeze blew bumps and whispers through the air. I knew I was being paranoid. Yet, I still couldn't unclench my arms as I walked quickly down the path.

My mind was begging me to turn around, to make my way back to my dorm and make myself an instant coffee. However, I wouldn't give in to the irrational fear, pumping through me. No. This was ridiculous. Though snippets of that alleyway flashed in warning, the clangs, groans and gunshots could almost be heard now in the solitary darkness. "You're being stupid," I scolded myself. Quickening my pace, I power-walked down the path, passing Caspers. I had walked this path so many times before, admittedly never on a Saturday morning.

The whispers grew louder the closer I walked to Casper's

and I kept my head down. I knew they were shut, which meant that whoever was there wasn't a customer. The last thing I needed was to interrupt whatever shady conversations was being held behind the bushes of the cafe.

"Oh come on," a gruff voice whispered.

Someone scoffed.

"If I were you I would watch your tone."

I was about to pass by the entry doors, when the shadows moved again. I jumped, scurrying in front of the building. I didn't dare peer around the side, eyes doubling in size as a man scoffed. Whoever they were, they were arguing, their voices hushed whispers that grew louder as I tried to silently make my way back around the building and away from the men.

"Marcelo-"

"How do you know Marcelo?"

Oh my gosh. This was shadier than I had thought. My feet told me to move, to leave before I was caught, my mind however was buzzing with adrenaline. *A drug deal*, I thought. It had to be. I couldn't believe it! Quinn would never believe me either, nothing gossip worthy ever happened on campus!

Stepping back, I tried not to breathe. The distinctive crunch of a rock under my boot had my mouth falling open as I felt my stomach drop. The conversation fell silent. Crap. I pulled away from the wall, ready to make my getaway as quietly as possible, when they started arguing again.

"Marcelo will not be impressed that you are on campus grounds."

It was like a reality TV show, and I was the stupid girl who was about to get drugged and stolen in a white minivan. I needed to leave.

"Marcelo and his ridiculous rules."

I shuffled as quickly and quietly as I could away from the corner, out of sight from the two men. My breath hitching as

I made my way around the corner. I spun quickly and started to briskly stride away. I didn't want to draw attention to myself, however, I needed to get out of here, quickly.

"Walk away now and he'll track you down before you can crawl back to your street corner!"

My legs shook, throat closing as I realised there were footsteps. Fast footsteps.

The growl of frustration had my stomach twisting and water coming to my eyes. What had I gotten myself into!

"Oh fu-"

Whoever it was abruptly stopped. I knew they could see me now. It was as if I could feel their eyes on me. *Keep your head straight Roux,* I thought. *Just keep walking.*

"West! Wes... get back here!"

Feet slapping against the melted snow had me wobbling, the fear of someone nearing made my stomach flip as I tried to refrain from looking. The louder the footsteps grew, the more my knees shook and lips wobbled.

"West!"

Then someone was running past me, his eyes briefly met mine, widening as he took in my fearful face, his legs seeming to plant themselves in as his eyes moved from mine to whoever was behind us. As if time slowed, his shout had me spinning.

"No!"

A loud crack sounded, the man's arms wrapped around me harshly as I was pulled to the ground, something hard slashed my stomach. Looking up bewildered, the man's eyes found mine as he shook on top of me, pulling back to pale. I followed his eyes and nausea filled my stomach at the blood coating my shirt.

He huffed, reaching behind him before pointing a gun in the direction of the other man, who was no longer firing at the stranger, but instead had disappeared.

I looked back down, realisation sunk in as a scream fell out of my mouth. *I had been shot! Oh my gosh, there was blood- my blood!* I tried to scurry away from the man. *Oh shit. I was going to die. Oh my gosh.*

I couldn't breath, my chest tightening at the thought. I had never gotten to publish a book, never been able to sign a first copy. I couldn't even say goodbye to my mum or Quinn. *My mum! Oh my gosh.* Tears spilled over my eyes as I cried, the pain in my stomach doubling at the movement. I didn't try to move as spots invaded my vision. A panic attack. *Oh my gosh I was having a panic attack.*

I screamed, pain ripping through my stomach as I was lifted off the ground, bumping around as he started running. His lips had been moving, I couldn't understand his words. My ears were ringing, my head dizzy. I had to apply pressure. I pushed down on my stomach and gasped, the pain ripping through me again. I pushed harder, crying.

"Roux!"

My head snapped up, his eyes bewildered, as if he couldn't believe I was in his arms. He knew my name. How did he know my name?

The pain rippled over me as he continued running, throwing me around in his arms. I gasped, darkness invading my vision as I felt my head fill with an unfamiliar buzz. Pain ripping through my muscles.

He had said something else, I was sure, however, I couldn't hear him. I couldn't hear anything as I felt myself be quickly pulled unconscious.

CHAPTER 5

It only took a second after I opened my eyes, to realise how badly my head was pounding. My eyes squinted, it was so bright. I just wanted to go back to sleep. Whatever this headache was, I didn't want to deal with it right now. Yet, I forced my eyes open, the realisation that this bed was far more comfortable than mine knocked the breath out of my lungs.

The ceiling was bright white. Where was I? I threw myself up abruptly, heart racing accelerating. My head spun as I gripped the bed railing for support. My stomach felt as if it were on fire as pain rippled through me. I looked down at my hand. *A hand railing? Was I in a hospital bed?* The walls matched the ceiling, the leather lounge in the corner confused me. I had never been in a fancy hospital room such as this one. At least, I hoped it was a hospital room, otherwise I had no idea where I was.

Images flashed through my brain, an instant pulsating pain appearing just as quickly with them. Caspers and the men passed vividly as I gasped, ripping the sheets away from

MARCELO

my body, pulling at my gown, my skin feeling like fire as I hissed. *How bad was it?*

The small gauze pad stared back at me sarcastically, waves of confusion doubling as I took it in. The pain felt as if a knife was being driven into my side and yet…it looked as if i had been attacked by nothing more than a bee. I had been shot. I knew I had. *Oh my gosh.* I grimaced, the headache growing worse the more I tried to think about this morning.

Surely, there had to be a nurse call button. I reached around the bed. They would be able to tell me what happened, or perhaps they would know who the man was who brought me here. Surely, it would have been more beneficial for him to leave me on the footpath to bleed out… I had clearly seen him and his dealer, partner, whoever he was, doing what I was sure was a drug deal or something of the sort.

I pressed the button on the remote beside the bed that I hoped would alert the nurses. I realised, with even more confusion, that there was a wrapper and half empty bottle of water on the table beside the bed, as if someone had been here recently. *Oh gosh.* My mum. She was going to freak out. She would drag me back home! I would have to spend my days serving coffee at the diner! I prayed that whoever had been sitting there, was anyone but my mother. Perhaps Quinn had been called, she was one of my emergency contacts. I groaned as I grabbed the remote next to the wrapper, pointing it up at the TV.

I clicked the remote to change the channel before I quickly switched back.

'Local student gets shot on campus,' ran across the bottom of the screen. No. There was no fucking way! I turned the volume up as I pulled myself to sit in the bed, grimacing at the stinging. Please tell me this was a joke.

"…where local student, Roux Fallon, was allegedly shot."

The news reporter was on campus! I quickly looked at the channel, relaxing slightly as I saw that it was simply the local news. My mother wouldn't have seen it. Not that she ever watched the news anyway, however, I was glad there wasn't a chance of her breaking down my hospital door and threatening the life of every thug in the city.

At least they didn't put up a picture. Still, this was not going to go over well. Now not only was I certain that the whole student body would know who I was, they'd be sure to ask questions. *Oh my gosh, Quinn.* She was surely having a fit right now. It was only a matter of time before she came storming through the door, I was sure a string of explicit curses would be spilled from her mouth. It was a good thing there were several hospitals in the city, even if this one was bound to be the closest to the university… I huffed. She was going to cause a commotion, the last thing I wanted. If being plastered on the TV wasn't enough, I was sure rumours would already be spreading around campus, the last thing I needed was Quinn's dramatics to amplify the story.

I sighed, my eyes falling shut. When I opened them, I was taken back by the young, slender woman standing in the doorway.

"Hi Miss Fallon, I'm your personal nurse here in the private wing of the hospital," she mumbled, smiling as my eyes widened. *Private wing?* "I'm sure you have a lot of questions, is there anything-"

"Thank you, I can inform her from here," a deep voice said smoothly.

The nurse seemed to make herself even smaller at his words, giving a short nod before she smiled at me and stepped back from the doorway. Who the hell was that? I had to hold back some explicit language of my own, that I was sure would have tumbled out of my mouth as a very large, muscular man walked through the door. His shoes looked shiny and expensive, his pants seemed to be tailored perfectly. The button down dark blue shirt he wore encapsulated his toned shoulders and arms. It had been rolled to his upper forearm, showing off his tanned skin, which seemed to be wrapped in an intricate tattoo. I knew I had seen him before. Though he wasn't from the university. That I was sure of. Those eyes. I tensed in an attempt to not gasp. *Shit.* Those eyes. Those deep green eyes. Declan. Suddenly the smell of blood seemed to waft into the room, a wave of anxiety crashing down upon me. He had survived. I couldn't help but fear him slightly, he didn't look like the street thug that had laid bleeding in the alleyway three years ago. No. He looked far more put together. A completely different man. Who was he?

"Miss Fallon," his honeyed voice cooed. My eyes snapped away from his. His eyes seemed different. Brighter. His stubble was thick, as if it had been unshaven for a few weeks. My stomach dropped.

His hair was no longer buzzed, long thick strands tied into a high bun. Overall, he looked younger, less intimidating.

"You must be very confused," he sympathised, coming to sit on the comfortable looking chair beside my bed.

I tried to reply, my throat half closed, however as his eyes met mine, I couldn't form any words. His green eyes bore into mine with enough emotion that my head started spinning. I couldn't believe it. His green eyes, the eyes of the injured man in the alley way watched me cautiously. I thought I was going to faint.

A knowing smile slowly etched onto his face.

"I really hope you remember me," he mumbled as he smirked down at me.

"Yes," I said quickly, trying to not seem as startled as I felt. *Why was he here? How did he know who I was?*

He smiled.

"Good. I feel terrible for thinking this, but I'm glad that morning hasn't slipped your mind." He sat back in his seat and sighed. "I'm here to apologise."

I had no idea what for. I had only met this man once before and I had assumed it would be the last. Before I could ask for clarification, his lips turned up slightly.

"It's a long story, however I think that is for another time. Although, I must admit that I'm feeling a little terrible, for being so thankful that our paths crossed again, even if it was under such disappointing circumstances."

Oh man. I pursed my lips, looking down, hoping the flushing of my cheeks wasn't obvious. I could feel the grin on his lips, begging me to look up and causing my cheeks to ache with a blush. I resisted smiling, this man was so, well, hot. And I was overwhelmingly confused by this whole situation. Not to mention embarrassed, from the tight knots that were forming in my stomach.

Why on earth did this have to happen to me? I didn't have time for any of this. I was meant to be at home working on my assignments, I was going to fall so behind.

I looked up as he cleared his throat, his confident eyes meeting mine quickly, he seemed to be waiting for a response. What was I meant to say to that? I didn't know this man, I didn't understand why he was here or what was happening and he was being so, so casual?

"If...um, you don't mind me asking," I took in a quick breath, trying to reel some of my confidence back in, "Well, why on earth am I in a private wing of the hospital, who are you, why are you here and what do you have to apologise for?"

I was sure it had come out harsher than I had intended, however, I also didn't really care. If he wanted to sit in here and act all suave while I laid in a hospital bed, I deserved answers. He looked at me a little shocked, his eyes wide and lips pursed. I was glad I had gotten his attention, this situation was far from funny to me, I had no idea what I had gotten myself into.

He seemed to ponder on my question for a moment before he answered.

"My name is Declan Marcelo," he said slowly, seeming thankfully, a lot less casual. "I'm a criminal lawyer and," he seemed to not know how to explain, pausing and looking down. "One of my...clients, was involved in your incident."

I stiffened. *Incident? I had been shot.* It may not have been very bad, however, it very well could have been!

"I hope you understand, Miss Fallon, that I am so sorry for what happened," he said. I couldn't care less for his apologies at the moment. I needed answers. "The morning I was shot, I had agreed to meet one of my clients...partners. What I didn't know though was, they wanted to meet with me because they were unhappy with my work." He took a deep breath. "It was a set-up, obviously. Regardless, the man who shot me was dealt with, not that I really cared at that point in time, all I could seem to think about was how lucky I was that you were there." My cheeks flushed. "I was notified of who you were by the police when they took my statement. I promised myself that I would repay you whenever I got the chance."

Oh my gosh. Surely the police weren't allowed to do that. No. They weren't.

"What?" I stuttered. This was all sounding ridiculous.

"You were never meant to get hurt. At least not when it had anything to do with me or my associates."

"Well, that sounds sketchy," it came out before I could stop it but the only part I regretted was that it sounded so juvenile. It did indeed sound, extremely sketchy.

His booming laugh filled the room quickly as he looked at me in disbelief.

"Well, yes, I guess it does." He laughed.

"A lawyer," I mumbled. He didn't look like a lawyer. His tattoos peeked from underneath his shirt and his hair seemed far from professional.

"Technically I'm the CEO of the Marcelo Firm downtown," he smirked. CEO? He looked far too young to be a lawyer, let alone run a firm.

"How old are you?" I asked, his dimpled smile grew bigger.

"I'm twenty eight, Miss Fallon."

Miss Fallon. I wasn't sure anyone other than my teachers had ever called me that. It seemed so different coming from his mouth. I most definitely shouldn't have been allowing the knots in my stomach to tighten from his tone. I forced a smile, my cheeks flushing.

"That's a little young to be running a company," I said. His smirk grew as he sat forward in his seat.

"And the way you're looking at me, Miss Fallon," he mumbled, "is a little too tempting for a hospital room."

My breath hitched and my face grew hot. My lips drew into a thin line. I didn't know this man.

"How old are you?" He smirked.

I shivered under his look.

"Twenty three."

He leant back in his seat, smirking while watching me with his intense gaze. The air felt thick as I tried to breathe, the hair on my arm standing straight as my body buzzed under the tension. I shouldn't be feeling like this, I didn't want to be. He may have been alluring but he was still a complete stranger to me. I wasn't going to feel such things for someone I had just met, someone I wasn't even sure if I trusted yet. This whole thing was a puzzle that I couldn't put together. I tried to sit up properly, I needed to ask him to leave. I needed space to think all of this through, to call Quinn and ask her to get me out of here.

As I tried to push myself up, Declan's hand sat gently on my shoulder, the heat from them halting any further movements.

"As minor as your wounds were Miss Fallon, you're still in a delicate position right now, and it's my job to make sure that you are alright." His features seemed so concerned as he gently pushed me back to the bed. I couldn't believe this guy. He hardly knew me, why on earth would he be concerned?

"I think you'll find that's the nurse's job," I breathed, I was sure he could feel it fan across his cheek from where he stood above me. I could smell the mint in his breath. I needed him to leave, so that I could breathe properly. He seemed to suck all the air out of the room with his presence. I could see why he was a lawyer.

"I think you should leave," I whispered.

A short laugh burst out of his mouth.

"This is my personal hospital suite Roux, I will leave when I know that you are safe."

Oh gosh. I was in his personal room?

"However, if it makes you feel better, I will go and wait in the waiting room, this shouldn't take much longer," he smiled before slowly walking to the door, turning briefly to glance at me before he left. As the door was shut, I felt my shoulders relax and I could finally breathe. I needed to figure out who he was and why I was in his room.

CHAPTER 6

Three hours...three hours of being stuck awake. Three hours of non-stop thinking over who Declan Marcelo was, all while being prodded and poked with needles and asked to pee into a cup. I had almost died when they had handed me a small plastic tube and asked for the latter, while Declan had been in the room. The visible pink tinge to his cheeks as he had quickly dismissed himself would forever be engraved in my brain. As would the burning of my own. Of course, that wasn't the most embarrassing part. The most embarrassing moment was when they had removed my gauze to check my stitches and I had finally gotten to see my bullet 'wound'. The hole was no bigger than my pinky fingernail, held together by what looked like two stitches and I had wanted to crawl up in a ball and cry at how dramatic I had thought it was. It did hurt, I wanted to reassure them, I hadn't thought I was dying for no reason!

My face had burned hotter than I thought possible, when the nurse had tried to reassure me that *even a minor gunshot wound could be dangerous.* I was pretty sure I had more chances of getting taken out from a grazed knee. I had no idea why I hadn't been discharged earlier. It was even worse, when I had asked about the removal of the bullet, and she had informed me that it had barely broken the skin, that it had merely grazed me.

Now I was stuck, sitting on the edge of my bed with a flat phone, no way to contact Quinn and ask her to come pick me up and wondering how on earth I was meant to get back to my dorm. I didn't exactly carry cash, my card was on my phone, which this morning at least had enough charge to last me until I finished my studying. *Ugh my studying*. I couldn't afford to fall behind.

"Ah Miss Fallon," the nurse mumbled as she walked through the door, my name didn't sound as nice coming from her lips, her face buried in a clipboard. She was probably as sick of me being here as I was.

"Your blood and urine tests have come back and everything seems fine, I just have a few things I need to go over before you can go."

I nodded, hoping to get this over with quickly. The longer I was in here, the more expensive my medical bill and I doubted I would like the number.

"You shouldn't try and lift anything heavy." She sighed. "No strenuous activities, short walks will do you good with the healing side of things…" her words seemed to drone on as she smiled. "Other than that you should be able to go about your day as normal. If there is an increase in pain after your medication or anything seems wrong, don't hesitate to book a check-up. The stitches should be dissolved in a week or two."

"Thank you," I forced a smile, she seemed nice enough.

Nodding at me and returning the smile, she wasted no time in turning and walking out of the room. She probably had a dozen other patients like me waiting to be taken care of.

I quickly collected my things and grabbed the bag that my clothes were in, quickly walked to the connecting bathroom. I frowned as I pulled my shirt over my head, the horrible red splotch on the front standing stark and obvious. I pulled my jacket tighter. I couldn't wait for a shower. My flat phone was shoved into the back pocket of my jeans, my book bag slung over my shoulder. The missed calls from Quinn were going to be endless. There was no doubt she would have seen the news. She was probably one minute away from back handing some hospital staff.

I froze as I opened the door, Declan staring at me with an easy smile.

"Miss Fallon."

"Declan," I regarded him, as I checked I hadn't left anything behind, picking up my book bag from beside the bed as my stomach pinched.

He smirked. That smirk. No, I didn't know him, he seemed off and I wouldn't let myself find him attractive.

"It's time to get you home," he said as he pulled the book bag from my arms. Oh my gosh. He was taking me home. *Oh please let him just order me a taxi, I couldn't sit through the drive to my campus next to him and keep my composure.* The air buzzed with tension around us, as we walked to the elevators. He seemed unaffected however, his calm and collected smile making me more uneasy. I should thank him, I realised, for letting me use his room.

"There's no need to worry about the paperwork," I jumped slightly as his voice echoed abruptly in the small space. "I've already sorted it for you." My stomach flipped at his words and I tried not to think about the fact that there was no way that this was allowed.

"You really didn't have to do that," I mumbled, as I fiddled with my hands.

I wasn't sure how he knew my details to fill out my forms,

I wasn't even sure it was legal, however he was a lawyer after all, I doubted he would do anything too out of the ordinary.

"Nonsense." He laughed. "Like I said before, my client brought you into this mess, this wouldn't have happened and without you I wouldn't be standing here today. I owe you much more than this." I didn't question him further, he seemed sure of his actions. Instead, I took the advantage of the mirrored walls, and snuck a glance at him. He was no doubt, very good looking. I felt bad for thinking it, when something about him seemed so odd, however, there was no denying it. If circumstances had been different, I probably would have been a blushing mess trapped in the elevator with him. Not to mention the way he spoke, with in such certainty and elegance. Any woman would be entranced by him.

"Oh, and you don't need to worry about the cost of this whole thing either." He rushed out. "I've taken care of it."

My stomach twisted in knots and I felt the guilt start to fill me up. He didn't have to pay my medical bills, no matter who I was to him.

"No Declan, I-"

"It's non-negotiable, Roux," he mumbled, the elevator doors opening. "Consider it a thank you gift."

A thank you gift? I had done what almost every other person would have done in that situation. He didn't need to do anything to repay me for that. All I had done was call an ambulance.

"I would prefer if I could pay you back for the bills," I mumbled. I didn't want to seem ungrateful, however there was no way I was letting him pay.

"I would prefer if you didn't." He smirked.

I was about to argue, when a tall man in a nurses outfit stepped in front of us. He reeked of sanitiser and I tried not to wrinkle my nose.

"Sign here please, Miss Fallon." He smiled professionally as he handed me the clipboard and pen. It still didn't sound as enticing as when it came out of Declan's mouth. I signed the dotted line, not bothering to read the document and handing him back the pen and board. Declan had filled it out, a lawyer, I was sure it was all done to standard.

Declan didn't hesitate to grab my arm and tug me gently away from the nurse, towards the door.

"I'll drop you back at your dorms." He smiled, pushing the door open for me.

I tried not to grimace. I was half-expecting him to have a personal chauffeur waiting for us as we exited. He seemed very much like the rich playboy type. However, no car was out the front of the hospital, not even a taxi and I realised that he was probably going to take me back to my dorm in his car. That I was in fact going to have to sit next to him and make small talk for the short drive back. I tried not to grimace. I wasn't much of a small talker, especially not to, super-hot, rich enough to have their own personal hospital suite men. I couldn't exactly argue with him though, so I nodded. It wasn't like I had any other choice. I would have to suck it up and try not to pass out from the awkward tension between us.

He walked with confidence beside me, as he led me to the passenger side door of a silver sports car on the curb. *Definitely rich,* I couldn't help but think. Not that it mattered, however he was obviously trying to flaunt it. This definitely wouldn't blend into the dorm car park, as if I wasn't going to have enough attention on me already from the news. *Ugh, the news.* I had forgotten about that little detail. Campus was going to be awful. The last thing I liked was eyes on me and now I was sure that they wouldn't stop following me. *Roux Fallon, the girl who managed to get shot on her way to get a coffee.*

I was surprised as he opened the door for me, however, I

tried to hide my smile and quickly scooted into the leather interior. I couldn't help but wonder how in less than twenty four hours, I had gone from walking to a coffee shop, to being driven home from hospital in a fancy car by a hot lawyer. A hot lawyer whose life I had saved. If it wasn't so ridiculous, I would have found it hilarious.

As he opened his door, smoothly sliding into his seat and throwing on some sunglasses, I felt the air in the car grow thick. His presence was something I wasn't sure someone could get used to. The intensity in his gaze as he looked at me didn't help. I wanted to scold myself for enjoying it slightly. however, allowed myself to indulge for a short moment, in the fact that someone so attractive would look at me in such a way. *Why oh why, did he have to be so good looking, when I would most probably never see him again.* I wasn't even sure why I wanted to see him again, I hardly ever grew attracted to people I didn't know. Even Zach didn't seem so attractive to me and I had been involved with him for months. I tried not to let myself overthink it though. He was an attractive guy, I couldn't help that. I could enjoy his looks for a moment, it wasn't as if he was ever going to be a distraction. Once he dropped me off and I could speak with him about the hospital bill, we would go our separate ways and this would all become a distant memory.

"I really am truly sorry that this happened to you, Roux," he mumbled, as he frowned at the road ahead.

My heartbeat quickened, his words sounding sincere.

"It's not your fault," I said looking away.

His frown deepened.

CHAPTER 7

The car was tense with silence. The radio was off, no music playing as we drove towards campus. The morning traffic had made the trip longer, dragging out the agony of my awkward inability to speak. It felt as if I was going to crawl out of my skin. I should have just listened to my gut and not gotten up early for the stupid study group. Honestly, what had I been thinking?

The tension only grew thicker the more I thought about it. My small frame pressing tightly against the door of the car. I probably looked like a complete idiot, but I would prefer to look like an idiot than have to look at him. The lingering feeling that this was far more than a coincidence and that us meeting again like this danced around the territory of fate, had me on edge.

The brief glances I stole, showed that he looked calm and collected. His green eyes watching the road cautiously in the slippery weather, seeming completely concentrated as he drummed his fingers against the steering wheel, humming the tune of a song I didn't know. Of course he would be calm. He didn't have anything to be worried about, unlike me. My face was now plastered over the local news, Quinn was probably two seconds away from spontaneous combustion, I had to try and find a way to keep this whole ordeal from my mother and I was now somehow in debt to a man who resembled a Greek god. All this, because I wanted a bloody coffee.

I honestly couldn't decide if I was angry at the fact that I had been brought into this whole mess, or unnerved about us meeting again. I couldn't help but feel a little lucky though, as he oozed confidence beside me, as if he had no worries in the world. It was suffocating, in an oddly pleasant way. The kind of way that had my stomach dropping and butterflies fluttering, making it hard to keep my breath steady. *Why had I met him, after all this time?*

It didn't help that I felt terrible. It wasn't that I thought he wouldn't be able to pay for my medical bills easily, he obviously could. It was the fact that he thought that he owed me something, that he was doing this because he felt he had to, that made my stomach ache.

I stole another quick glance over, his eyes capturing mine as he peered back questioningly.

"Is there something wrong, Miss Fallon?" he asked.

My throat bobbed. *Yes, I wanted to scream.*

"No," I mumbled, as I turned away, the familiar hot blush creeping up my neck to settle in my cheeks.

"Are you sure?"

I couldn't respond, his arm making its way around me and across the top of my seat, the heat radiating off silencing me as I shivered. I realised how cold I was as I felt the warmth hitting the back of my neck, winter in the city was harsh and today was no different.

"Miss Fallon?"

I half-heartedly cleared my throat.

"Positive."

His laugh came out small and breathy in the tight space of the car, the movement causing his fingertips brushing my shoulder. I couldn't help but tense, goosebumps rippling down my spine and rolling over my shoulders.

"Perfect," he whispered, his attention returning to the road. The air in the car was hard to breathe, having grown incredibly thicker with our interaction.

I needed to ask him how exactly he knew so much about me. Why he was doing all this when he had only met me once and why he felt the need to after three years of no contact. However, nothing would come out other than a sigh, as he pulled his arm back to change the gears.

"I'm very glad we crossed paths again, Roux."

His voice had grown to a deep rasp. It sadly sounded delicious and I felt my nerves spike again. If only he knew the effect he was having on me, he may have toned down the suaveness. I wished he would, this situation was complicated enough without his attractiveness. Clearing my throat, I peered up at him.

"Me too."

It was a shock to my system, when I realised I actually wasn't lying. I was glad we had met, I had gotten some closure as to how he was, although the circumstances were enough to make me put off with his reappearance. Especially as he chuckled, his eyes crinkling as he seemed unaffected yet again by the tension. I wasted no time in snapping my gaze back to the window, my eyes doubling in size as I saw my university campus.

My campus was correct, however, the dorm building that stood tall in front of us was not mine, rather the dorms that I had dropped Quinn off at countless times before to see William. I couldn't blame Declan for dropping me off at the fancy dorms, they were the easiest ones to access from the street and he probably didn't even realise that there were others, however, this didn't stop the blush creeping over my cheeks as he stepped out of the car. I didn't want to have to tell him that he had driven me to the wrong dorms. Sighing, I opened the car door, step-in into the cold air as my breath was taken away.

Declan was beside me in a matter of seconds, his hand on my lower back gently pushing me towards the doors and out of the freezing air.

"I'll walk you to your dorm." He smiled as we walked towards the entrance. I didn't have a choice but to tell him that I didn't live here. These were the recently renovated buildings and only the upper class students, such as Will and Susie lived here.

"I...um, well, my dorm is on the other side of the campus."

He looked at me for a moment before a smile appeared on his face. His hair flopped about as he shook his head, laughing down at me.

"Not anymore."

I stared at him confused, his knowing smirk peering back at me. My heart began to race in my chest. *No. What had he done?*

"What?" I asked, hoping he was joking.

He smirked.

Oh my gosh. No.

"That's...this is too much," I stuttered as I looked at the building in front of me. He couldn't be serious.

He rolled his eyes as he began walking to the doors. I had no choice but to walk with him. How did he not think that this was a huge deal?

"Declan," I muttered guiltily, as he powered into the building.

"The chairman mentioned that the press were all over your old dorm room and agreed to a change."

"Chairman?"

Declan turned, eyeing me confused.

"Yes, I'm one of the major sponsors for the law department, I was notified of the incident. Of course due to the situation Mr Thox more than agreed to a change."

This was ridiculous. "I really don't mind about some cameras, this is a bit much. None of this was actually your fault and even if it was, I wouldn't expect this."

He spun quickly, one foot on the staircase and the other watching me incredulously.

"You saved my life Roux," he said. His eyes held a fiery intensity as they stared down at me. "I owe you everything, this isn't up for discussion."

I had no idea what to say after his outburst. I knew I couldn't possibly accept this, yet he was looking at me with such intensity that I kept my mouth shut. It was obvious he had made up his mind and he didn't seem as though he was going to change his decision. Little did he know my mind was also made and there was nothing he could say or do to make me keep this dorm.

Oh my gosh. Had he had the administration students move my things? I didn't even want to think about what they found. My old comfortable underwear came to mind and I wanted the ground to swallow me up then and there.

I may have saved his life once, however, I had hardly thought about this man for the past three years. For him to show up so unexpectedly and thank me with such an expensive invasion of privacy...my conscience would never recover.

"I can't," I said with finality as he walked further up the stairs.

"Good thing, it's already paid for," he said without looking back, making his way briskly up the staircase. I had no choice but to follow.

CHAPTER 8

"You...it's what?" I nearly screamed as I pushed myself up the staircase. I could almost feel the roll of his eyes as he dramatically turned to look at me.

"Miss F-"

"Roux?" My gaze snapped to Will, who stood cautiously on the floor above us, watching Declan with an interrogative gaze. "Is everything alright here?" he asked, eyes bouncing between Declan and I before settling big-brotherly like on me.

I was glad that I had such good friends, however, at this moment in time I wanted nothing more than to throw William down the stairs. No it was not okay but not because Declan wasn't being polite, more so that he was being too nice and that pissed me off.

"Yes Will." I sighed as I walked around Declan. "It's a long sto-"

"Don't you dare say it's a long story Roux!" Will scolded as he peered at Declan, pulling me carefully in front of his wide shoulders in an attempt to block his view.

His eyes returned to mine and widened like saucers.

"Roux!" he whispered harshly as he scanned me up and down. "The news, are you, I mean-"

I cut off his stuttering as I rolled my eyes.

"Don't believe everything you hear on the news Will, I'm fine," I mumbled, trying to peer around him to make sure Declan was still there. We weren't finished having this argument.

"But-"

"Look I'm really sorry but we've got to go and it is a long story, Will," I rushed, cutting him off as I motioned for Declan to keep following me up the stairs. I had no idea what level this 'new dorm' was on. However, as I peered up the winding staircase I realised just how many it had. *Please don't let me be on the top*, if this was anything like a hotel the further up I was the more expensive it was.

Declan quickly overtook me and sped up the staircase at an annoyingly fast pace. Roughly halfway up, I realised he had started walking down the hallway instead of up the other flight of stairs. There didn't seem to be many rooms on each floor, maybe three. It made me nervous, surely they couldn't be that much bigger than a normal dorm. Yes they had been renovated, but they were still a part of my campus, and our university wasn't exactly the best of the best.

I stopped abruptly, almost running into Declan's back as he motioned for the wooden door closest to the end of the hallway.

"Your new room," he said, pulling a key from his back pocket.

The door swung open, a small white entryway beckoned me to go inside, however, I stood still, despite the aggravating excitement bubbling throughout me and faced Declan.

"I can't accept this," I said again, my patience growing thin. I wasn't sure if it was because I was exhausted and just wanted to go and sleep in my old dorm room or because the lavish entry looked like it belonged to a fancy apartment in the city and not a dorm room, however, whatever it was, it left me feeling on edge and prickly. I wanted him to stop looking at me with his stupid smirk, I wanted to go and find Quinn and get a hug. Not go into a dorm room which I couldn't possibly accept, only to appease Declan's guilt.

I was surprised that Declan didn't drag me into the room, instead choosing to roll his eyes at me and take a step back.

"I have a meeting that I need to get to at the firm, so unfortunately I can't stay and chat to you about this whole situation." He smirked. "However, your things should have been moved and you'll find everything you need inside."

I sighed ready to protest when I saw him walking backwards down the hallway.

"Declan!" I exclaimed. He couldn't possibly just think that he could leave!

"If you need anything or you have any trouble just call me," he smiled.

I wanted to stop him but he started jogging down the stairs at record pace. Looking back at the open door I sighed. This was completely ridiculous.

As I walked in, I realised just how modern they had made these dorms. They were beautiful to say the least. Well, as beautiful as a dorm room could get. The small entryway was simple and plain, with hardwood floors and white walls. The sitting area was next, the decent sized lounge, that I had most definitely not bought, looked funny across from my small TV. Marble bench tops gleaned from the kitchen, my stomach turning in jealousy of Will and his dorm room. I now understood why we had only ever hung out in mine or Quinn's. If this was anything like mine, I wouldn't want to show it off to us either. The door next to the pantry must have led to the bedroom.

If anything, this open style dorm screamed inner city apartment, I loved it. The daffodils on the table caught my eye, however, I chose to ignore them, knowing they must have been from him. Just like the rest of this was. I felt bad for enjoying it so much. I wasn't staying, I was sure of that. No matter how wonderful the dorm was, or how sure he had been of his gift, I knew I could never accept this.

I would have to go down and speak with the administration's desk about arranging a change back to my old dorm. However, first I would need to find my charger and plug in my phone so that I could message Quinn, she was surely stressed by now. After I spoke with the administration I would have to go explain this whole situation. I also knew I needed a shower, I looked like a wreck.

I dragged my feet to the door I was sure was the bedroom, I realised just how exhausted the day had left me, my stomach ached and my legs were wobbly. However, I didn't have time to feel sorry for myself, I needed to get this sorted.

CHAPTER 9

I had assumed correctly and the door led to a large bedroom. I hoped the giant queen-sized bed came with all of these dormitories, like the single in my old room had. Otherwise, I knew the only other option was that Declan had gotten it put in himself. I wouldn't have been surprised. Inside the bedroom, however, there had been a small en-suite, not much larger than the one in my other dorm and I was thankful for the normalcy that it brought in size. My fuzzy turtleneck green sweater and tights comforted me as I ran over the plan in my head. *Speak with administration, organise a swap, move my stuff, go back to my old dorm.*

I shut the door behind me, pocketing the small key. It didn't take me long to run down the staircase to the administration desk, I had been sure to move faster on the second floor, gladly avoiding Will and his scrutinising gaze.

The entry room in the foyer was just as large as I remembered it, the administration desk sitting small in the corner. I was shocked to see the small woman sitting behind it, smiling sweetly up at me as I approached. She couldn't have been much older than me, my old dormitories admin had been a cranky middle-aged man named Kent. I was glad to see her welcoming face.

"Hi my name's Rouxette Fallon." I smiled, trying not to cringe at my name.

"How may I help you today Rouxette?" she asked politely as she sat her phone down on the table.

Where was I even supposed to begin?

"Well, I recently changed dorms," I started, she nodded along with me politely, her small lips curving into a smile. She was probably a student, like me. "I was hoping that I would be able to change back," I mumbled. She looked confused for a moment. " It's not that I don't like the new one!" I assured her. "I just wasn't expecting such a change."

Technically I wasn't lying, I hadn't expected such a change. However, I also hadn't expected a change at all. She continued nodding her head as she fumbled with the computer.

"Yes of course, I just need to double check that no one had replaced you in your old dorm room yet." She smiled. "When was the move?"

"This morning," I said softly, fiddling with my hands and hoping she could have this done soon. I just wanted to be back on my floor with Quinn, eating some crappy dinner and studying.

"Rouxette Fallon," she murmured, squinting at the computer. "You were in dorm 8 on floor G?"

"Yep."

Her frown startled me and she shook her head at the computer.

"Actually," she said slowly, looking up at me with an eyebrow raise. "It seems Chairman Thox has specifically asked for your change in dormitories…for your scholarship."

"There must be some mistake?" I frowned. "I don't have a scholarship."

She looked confused as her eyes returned to the screen, then back to me.

"I'm just going to call Chairman Thox and see what's going on, truly, I'm a little confused." She smiled.

I sighed and spotted the comfortable looking waiting chairs. I just wanted to sleep. She spoke low and fast on the phone with the chairman, the thunder that began outside had startled me as I tried to eavesdrop. I really should try and drop that habit.

My eyes began to droop as the rain started outside, the downpour causing me to become more tired than I already had been. If the door chime hadn't have gone off when it did, I was sure I would have fallen asleep in the chair.

The bald man in the doorway, wore a thick trench coat and eyed the room cautiously before his eyes fell on me.

"Mr Thox?" the lady behind the desk asked incredulously.

"It's fine Abigail." He smiled politely. "I thought it would be best to discuss things with Miss Fallon myself." His gaze found mine again and he stuck out a large hand for me to shake.

"I'm Chairman Thox," he said, as if I wasn't already aware. "It's lovely to meet you Rouxette, I cannot express how happy I am that we have you studying with us."

I wasn't sure how to respond.

"Thank you," I mumbled awkwardly, shuffling my feet. If only I were in my bed asleep.

"No need to be thankful Miss Fallon," he rushed, "I do hope our dormitories have been up to standard?"

"Of course, they're wonderful," I paused. This was so awkward. "That's actually what I wanted to get sorted."

He held the door open for me, as he ushered me into the

small meeting room to the side of the foyer. I hadn't even realised the door was there.

"Of course, I had assumed you would have some questions," he replied.

Where did I even begin?

"I would like to move back to my old dorm," I said shakily. He stared back at me, his forehead furrowing and my plans grew sweaty. "I'm not even sure-"

"Miss Fallon, I don't think you understand the full light of this situation." He smiled, as if he hadn't just cut me off.

"No, I don't," I replied clipped. As important as he was, he was also rude.

"Mr Marcelo has made it very clear as to the conditions of your scholarship," he started. "As well as the terrible publicity that would have been placed on the school if the press perceived your incident as dangerous."

I wanted to laugh. *It had been dangerous. I had been shot. Sort of.* I had no idea how to respond to his comment. My brain seemed like it was teetering on the edge of a mental breakdown and laughing fit. He seemed just as uncomfortable as I felt. Whatever he was getting at, I was sure I wouldn't like it.

"He very generously, decided to make a donation to the school in order for us to keep the press satisfied regarding your incident and to keep the details private." He said.

No way...no. This was all getting too complicated!

"The donation, however," he continued, "he made it very clear that it was not only to be used for the reporter's but also for a new scholarship program that he had been looking into funding."

No. I knew I wouldn't like it. There was no way I would ever accept such a thing.

He looked awkwardly strained, as if he was constipated as he continued,.

"He also put forward that perhaps you would be a great candidate, due to your circumstances and the fact that your incident happened on school grounds. After looking at your rankings, which are quite high I might add, we agreed that it might be best for you to be the first student to receive the Marcelo Firm Scholarship."

It felt as if my chest was tightening. I didn't want a scholarship. I didn't want this new room. It was as if Declan was taking over my life. He couldn't just come in and change everything. I wanted to stay on the same floor as Quinn! I wanted to have our sleepovers and movie nights! I wouldn't be forced to stay here, no matter how nice it was. Especially not, when the only reason he was doing this was because he felt bad.

"Miss Fallon?" Mr Thox asked.

"Sorry," I whispered, running my hands over my face, they felt tingly. I was buzzing, a mix of over tired and stressed. "I can't accept this scholarship."

His eyes bulged as he opened and closed his mouth. I didn't blame him, I was sure most students would jump at this opportunity. I knew why I was being offered this though and I couldn't accept.

"You what?" he sputtered.

"I can't accept this. I would like my old dorm room back and I do not need a scholarship, I am sure there are students who would love to take it off your hands, go and ask them," I said, standing from the uncomfortable seat. My body was begging me to go upstairs and lay down in the huge bed and fall asleep.

He sighed as he watched me, seeming conflicted.

"Mr Marcelo has made it very clear-"

"Are you telling me that I do not have a say in what happens to me on this campus?" I abruptly asked.

I was getting sick of all these males ordering me around

to do as they pleased so that they felt better. If they cared at all I would be allowed to go back to my old dorm, to my best friend and have a good cry about the events of today.

"No, no!" he rushed. "It's simply that this offer-"

"This offer is Declan's attempt to apologise for something that he doesn't need to," I said sternly. "And I will choose whether or not I will accept it. Which I have and that is to decline, thank you, Mr Thox." I huffed.

He looked frazzled, as if he wasn't sure how to proceed.

"I will see what I can do," he mumbled.

He stood quickly, not meeting my eye as he brushed his coat and held out his hand.

"Miss Fallon," he said. I stood, shaking his hand and smiled.

"Thank you, Mr Thox."

I followed him out of the small room, glad to be out in the open space of the foyer. He gave a small nod before he walked away, pulling out his phone. I wasted no time in turning back towards the stairs. If I was going to be stuck in this room for a little while longer, I was going to enjoy the big bed. Surely a nap wouldn't disrupt the change of dorms. *Then I can call Quinn,* I thought. My stomach dipped at the thought of not telling her I was okay sooner, however, my muscles wept for me to lay down.

The stairs were a mission in themselves, my legs feeling like jelly as I pushed myself forward. Stomping followed someone down as they ran my way.

"Rouxette Fallon!" *Quinn. Crap.* "You're dead!" she screamed, her eyebrows furrowed and face red as she ripped me off my feet into a tight hug.

"I was so worried!" Quinn screamed as she pulled away from me.

Her breath hit my face in ragged puffs as she looked me up and down.

"No one knew anything and the news, oh my gosh the news!" She gasped, eyes watering. "Everyone's saying you got shot, I couldn't get any information from any hospital!" she paused to draw in a breath.

"Quinn, breathe," I mumbled. "How did you know I was here?"

She looked offended as she threw her arms in the air, eyes narrowing.

"That is so not the point!" she screeched. "I'm your best friend and I had to get a call from Will saying that he saw you and some sketchy ass dude in his dormitory!"

Fucking Will, I was going to miss him when I killed him. I rolled my eyes at her dramatics and sighed as I started walking back up the stairs.

"Come up to my dorm and I'll explain."

"Your dorm!" she sputtered.

I huffed and closed my eyes as I tried to gather all the strength I had left as to not push her dumb ass down the stairs.

"It's a long story."

CHAPTER 10

Quinn's mouth hung open in disbelief, her hair a mess. She had remained silent for the last two minutes and I thought perhaps the world really had stopped spinning. Perhaps I should have held back some of the details of the story.

"So on a scale of one to ten how hot is he?" she asked.

I rolled my eyes but sighed.

"Quinn, he could very well be the love child of two Greek gods okay, he's a bloody ten."

"Oooooh." She giggled.

I knew I was only feeding her gossip addiction but what could I say after the day I had dealt with, I had the goods.

"I can't believe this." She laughed as she laid back on the bed. I felt like laughing with her as I shook my head.

"I know."

"Are you sure you're okay, you know with everything that's happened?" She asked. "I know that it's not that bad but if I were you I'd be pretty shaken up."

I paused, sighing.

"I'm not sure what I feel or how I am," I said as I slayed

back on the insanely comfortable bed. "But could you stay with me?" I asked as I looked over at her with the biggest puppy dog eyes I could muster. She scoffed and cuddled into my side.

"As if you need to ask." She laughed.

I smiled and closed my eyes as I felt my muscles start to loosen into the bed. After explaining everything, I realised how terrifying it actually was that I had basically been shot on school grounds. However, somehow my mind couldn't even be bothered to feel shocked. After everything with Declan and Chairman Thox I hadn't really had time to stop and think about it. Surely they would have put something in place, to stop this from happening again.

My phone's buzz drew me from my relaxation as it turned on. The relentless dinging of my notifications made me want to cringe.

"I hope that's all you." I sighed.

My mother couldn't find out about this. I had to make sure, at least until my graduation so I could move far away from here before she put me under house arrest.

She couldn't have heard about it from our hometown, that was a plus. I just had to hope that this hadn't warranted the university to call her.

"What are you going to do?" Quinn asked as she rolled onto her stomach.

"I'm going to figure out a way to give all of this back," I said simply.

She looked at me for a moment, sighing.

"I know where you're coming from babe, really. Do you really think the price of any of this matters though? Like he has his own private hospital room, he's obviously very well-off. Maybe you should think about the benefits of all of this. If he's doing this because he feels guilty maybe you should let him."

I could understand where she was coming from. It wasn't that simple though. It wouldn't be right to accept any of this and I didn't need more reasons to be connected to him.

"I can't."

I could almost feel her eye roll.

"I know." She laughed, looking around the room with a grin. "But whoa…"

I huffed a laugh as well.

"Yeah." I laughed.

Whoa. That was definitely the correct word to describe today, this room and just about anything that led to Declan. I couldn't believe Will had never had us over to his dorm, it would have been much more spacious than mine or Quinns. Of course, he may have had Quinn over, perhaps I was the third wheel in their little romance. Not that I could even be mad, we all knew Quinn and Will would undoubtedly end up together, if I could help speed up the process then I was all for it. They had been dragging on their friendship for far too long.

"Have you told your mum what happened?" she asked.

Why on earth would I have done that? Quinn knew how sensitive my mother was, if she knew that even a hair on my head had been harmed she would have a full on mental breakdown!

"No."

I wasn't sure if it was my tone or if Quinn could feel the tension growing in the room. However, she wasted no time in sitting up and pushing herself off of the bed.

"I'm gonna go and get a drink." She smiled. "You want one?"

"Please."

That was if whoever moved my stuff even thought about moving the contents of the shared kitchen fridge and if they pried enough to see what was labelled with my name.

"Girl, you do realise there's a vase of flowers sitting on your dining table with a note right?" Quinn called.

I tried not to grimace. *Ah yes, the daffodils.*

"Yeah."

I could hear her scoff from the kitchen, her sneakers tapping lightly on the floor as she held the letter up to me.

"So?" she asked, eyes wide in her usual dramatics.

My eyes rolled on their own accord.

"I'm not interested in whatever it says," I mumbled as my head hit the mattress again. It wasn't a complete lie. Yes, I wanted to know what on earth he could have possibly written on the note but no I didn't care what it actually said.

I heard the rip before I could spring up and Quinn held the note out in front of her, smiling like a child.

"Roux, ooooh even his writing looks hot." She smirked. *Idiot, it was probably the writing of some middle aged-woman behind the counter at the flower shop.* "I hope you will accept my attempt at an apology and a thank you. You deserve much more than a safer dorm for all that you have done for me, especially after what I have brought upon you. Most of your things should be moved by now, and arranged accordingly. Call me at any time with any questions, Declan Marcelo." Quinn stood mouth agape at the paper.

I couldn't blame her. My face flamed at the thought that some flower shop owner had to write that. That they had even heard it.

"Oh my gosh, Roux!" she squealed, flopping down beside me. "It's his number!"

Great.

"You so have to call him!" She grinned as she threw the paper at me, bouncing like a five-year-old at a fair. *No. There was no way I was calling Declan.* I didn't want to be distracted by him further. He had already made my nerving day more complicated and had refused to listen to me about the dorm.

If I was calling him, it would be to give him a piece of my mind.

"No Quinn."

She pouted and threw herself back on the bed. I couldn't help but crawl up to the covers and climb under. My body felt as if it was filled with rocks, slowly sinking further into the comfortable mattress.

I could feel Quinn squeeze-in beside me.

"You sure you're okay?" she whispered.

I just nodded my head, my mind already slipping into oblivion.

CHAPTER 11

"Do it," Quinn whined from the breakfast bar, as I flipped two eggs in the pan. No. I absolutely was not calling him. There was no way. "You never know, this call might be the one that gets your point across!"

I rolled my eyes, laughing at her.

"Please, you just want me to call him so you can hear his voice," I teased.

"Duh!" she yelled.

I was glad I wasn't going to have to get used to the echo in the large room.

"It's probably a sexy ass voice!" She laughed.

It was. However, I was not going to randomly call him and demand that he take all of this back. At least not for Quinn to get a good earful of his voice. I had already spoken to the chairman. There was nothing more I had to do. This would all be sorted soon.

"No," I said firmly with a smile, as I turned back to cooking.

I smirked, ignoring her huffing as I grabbed two plates. I was glad that whoever had moved my things had grabbed my food from the kitchen fridge, everything seemed to be in there. However, sitting inside the large fridge without anyone else's food, I realised I may need to go grocery shopping sometime soon, it didn't look like much.

I handed the plate over to her, jumping as my phone began ringing from the bench top. The number was displayed on the screen and I couldn't help but frown at the unknown number. No one usually called me, unless it was my mother or grandparents. I could only hope it was the chairman with good news.

I silently pressed the answer button, Quinn looked at me confused as I walked out of the kitchen.

"Hello?" I asked, walking in and shutting the bedroom door.

"Miss Fallon…"

My breathing hitched, there was no way this was happening. Why was the universe against me?

"Declan?" I breathed out, trying to regain my composure.

The door flung open behind me, hitting the back of my head. I couldn't help the curse that flew from my mouth.

"Are you okay?" Declan asked quickly. *No*, I wanted to say. *I'm about to die from embarrassment.*

"It's him!" Quinn whisper-yelled as she jumped around me, grin growing bigger as I tried to hit her.

"Yeah I'm all good, sorry, just dropped something," I said, as I picked up the pillow off the bed and flung it at Quinn, a scowl prominently growling at her on my face.

"Yeah your dignity!" she whispered from across the room. That idiot needed to calm down.

"Oh okay, well, I'm sorry for interrupting your morning, however I received quite a distressed call from Chairman Thox."

I could almost hear the smirk in his voice.

"Okay…" I said.

"I don't suppose you had something to do with that?" he asked as Quinn motioned for me to put the phone on speaker. I rolled my eyes but followed her demand.

"I've already told you Declan, I can't accept this."

"Miss Fallon," he said smoothly, I could see Quinn's mouth hang from beside me and I tried not to laugh at her. "You saved my life and I put yours in danger-"

"But how?" I cut him off. "It's not like you're the one who shot me," I fired back.

He sighed.

"Roux, I would rather not have this conversation over the phone, why don't we go out for dinner so that we can properly talk this through?"

He asked the question so casually that I wasn't sure I had heard him right. Quinn was silently screaming in front of me, seemingly excited at his offer.

"I would rather get this sorted now," I said coolly.

I avoided Quinns widening eyes. Declan's chuckle seemed to distract her briefly, as she flopped onto the bed fanning her face dramatically.

"Of course you would." He laughed. "So what exactly is the problem?" he asked.

"The problem, Declan, is that I can't accept a brand-new dorm and scholarship just because you have some pent-up guilt over what happened, we hardly know each other-"

"I'm definitely not offering you all of this because of guilt, Roux, I wasn't kidding when I said I owe you everything, without you I wouldn't be standing here today and I promised myself three years ago that if I ever got the chance I would repay you the best way I could. The dorm is a good start, as for the scholarship, I figured my corporation could benefit from doing something different."

I wasn't sure what to say, my stomach twisted in knots at the thought of what happened three years ago. I could understand why he would want to repay me, but why didn't he understand? I didn't want him to!

"Im sorry Declan," I mumbled awkwardly. "I'm not accepting the scholarship."

There was a small pause, I thought perhaps I had pissed him off enough that he would agree.

"Breakfast in the morning, your choice of café, we can talk about negotiations."

Such a lawyer. He didn't seem like the type to give up, however he obviously didn't know who he was talking to.

"I have a lecture," I smirked. It wasn't a lie. "I'll talk to Chairman Thox again about all of this then, because regardless of your connections you can't make me stay here or accept the scholarship," I laughed lightly, hoping he wouldn't be too offended by my bluntness. "Thank you for your help, Declan, I hope we can come to an understanding."

The line went silent as I hung up.

I didn't have time to look up before I was being flung into the bed, Quinns squealing ringing in my ears as a pillow was rammed into my face. Her voice was muffled by the pillow, however, her words were clear.

"You idiot!" I couldn't get the pillow off of my face as I wriggled and thrashed underneath her. "Absolute moron!" she continued. "You could have had a date!"

The thought was laughable. It wasn't that I hadn't been on a date before, or been with a guy before. I had a long-term relationship before, a lovely one, now though. As if I would waste my time on a date, let alone a date with Declan Marcelo to speak about negotiations for an offer I had clearly declined multiple times.

"Get off!" I tried to scream, my words muffled in my own ears. Quinn just groaned louder as she lifted the pillow. I drew in a deep breath before the air was stopped by the pillow hitting my face.

"Idiot!" She huffed, throwing the pillow down beside us.

"Are you done?" I asked breathlessly as I looked at her red face.

A scowl greeted me, causing me to grin, such a drama queen.

"Yes," she grumbled as she slipped off of me. "I still can't believe you turned him down," she frowned as she gave me a look of confusion. My eyes lulled around as I tried not to laugh at her.

"It wasn't like that."

She just rolled her eyes and huffed.

"Were both going to turn into old ugly cat ladies," she mumbled disappointedly. A laugh bubbled from my lips.

"I love cats."

Quinn just scowled.

CHAPTER 12

My stomach twisted, the looks and questions I was sure to get from other students this morning had already put me on edge. The comfortable bed did nothing to ease the knots growing in my belly. I was fairly sure I had about two minutes before my alarm would go off to tell me to get ready for my lecture. However, the thought of getting up, had my mind spinning in such a state already that I knew it was going to be a terrible day.

I was disappointed that Quinn had to leave early for her drama group, at least if she was with me I wouldn't have to make the awkward walk to English class by myself. I was sure that by now everyone had heard what happened and wouldn't waste a second in asking me about the incident. At least I would have the cover of Hannah and Susie in the lecture, even though we weren't close, I was sure they would know better than to pry into things they don't belong in.

The hair on my arms stood straight as my alarm blasted through the room. The thought of having to leave the warm cocoon of my blankets had my face buried deep into my pillow, a groan slipping from my lips. *Here we go again,* I thought. *Back to reality.*

I wouldn't have been surprised if my phone had cracked as I slammed down on the stop button. As I threw the covers off and the cold air hit my skin, I doubted I would have cared either. I needed a coffee, however that would have to wait until I showered and cleaned my wound. I wasn't sure how they had expected me to shower without getting the gauze wet, I had no choice but to stick my limbs under the water one by one.

When I was finished, I didn't bother waiting for the jug to completely boil, downing my warm coffee in seconds before pouring another to sip as I got dressed. Everything ached, my arms were like jello by my sides, my legs as stiff as a dry sponge. It didn't help, the ointment for my 'wound' seemed to only make it sting even worse.

However, the worst part of my morning by far was the realisation that I now had to walk across campus to get to my classes, meaning that I didn't have time to do my morning revision. If Declan had just let me deal with this myself, this never would have been happening. None of this was as helpful as he thought. If I had stayed in my old dorm last night, I would have been quicker to my classes and less likely that I would have run into any other issues along the way.

As I picked my phone and keys up, my eyes widened at the time. I had half an hour to get to my lecture, roughly the same time it took to get there. I was never late for classes. This was ridiculous. Perhaps if I cut across the fields, I could make it in twenty minutes, of course I wasn't risking that in the early morning. I'd rather be late and stick to the main path than risk coming across something again.

I made sure to lock the dorm room door before I left, the last thing I needed was someone breaking in before I could leave. Knowing my luck they would put a hole in the wall or something and I would be forced to stay here. I thought it surprising that a building of this size didn't have an elevator, even my old dorm rooms had a rickety one that was almost always broken. I wasn't sure how anyone on the higher levels could handle the walk up and down the staircases.

"Roux!"

I spun, locking eyes with a confused Will. His eyes seemed to roam over me in a brotherly way, assuring him that I was okay. I was glad to have Will most of the time, he was like the brother I never had, today though, was not one of those days.

I couldn't help the groan that whined from my lips.

"Not today Will," I drawled.

He looked at me incredulously as he put his hands up in the air.

"What the fuck is going on?" he asked, confused.

Then I was in a hug, a tight one. I tried not to wince as he squeezed, my stomach aching.

"What happened, are you okay, who the hell was that asshole with you yesterday?"

There were so many questions he was firing that I didn't get a chance to answer any of them, instead resorting to slapping my hand over his mouth and sighing.

"I'm fine, the news made it sound far worse than it was, it's just a scratch," I assured him. "The guy is a long story but I'll explain later, or ask Quinn, I'm sure she can fill you in." I smiled.

"Roux, you can't just disappear for a day, get your face plastered all over the news and expect me to just drop this!" he scolded, arms folded over his chest.

I sighed, eyes drooping shut while I rubbed a hand slowly over my face.

"I'm sorry, Will, honestly I'm just as confused about all of this as you are, but I'm really late for class," I tried to reason.

His face became even more confused and I could basically see all the little wheels in his head turning.

"Why are you here?" he asked, scrunching up his face.

I couldn't help but groan.

"It's a long story, I'll fill you in later, I promise!" I rushed as I tried to get away. "Or really just ask Quinn!" I called and started rushing towards the never-ending stairs.

"Be safe, call me after class!" I heard him call quickly. I did feel bad for not explaining things further, but what was I supposed to say? *Oh yeah, well you know that guy I found in an alleyway three years ago, yeah his back and is buying me heaps of expensive things because I managed to get shot on my way for a coffee.* yeah, I didn't think so.

I wasted no time in flinging the glass doors open and running out. The chilly morning air took me by surprise causing my breath to catch. I didn't have any time to waste though, as I started power-walking down the path, trying not to draw any attention to myself as the mass of students mingled about.

It was easy enough to wind my way through them, no one seemed to pay any attention to me, just like any other day and I thanked myself for being average. I was surprised it hadn't started snowing yet in the city weather. Usually by this time of year the clouds would be forming overhead and the grounds would be covered in slippery white snow. Students would be throwing snow balls at each other and I would be dodging their aim of fire every five minutes. I was glad that the cold had come late this year.

It wasn't until I had gotten to the halls of my lecture building that my invisibility wore off. My shoulder rammed into something, the sharp pain had me hissing as I stumbled backwards. Zach.

"Roux," he said, eyes wide. "You're okay?"

"Yes?" I mumbled, he sounded almost shocked.

His big doe eyes and frown made for a killer apologetic look and if I didn't know how much of a turd he was, I might have found it attractive. However, in the moment the look of pity had my mind spinning with embarrassment and I wanted nothing more than to slap him and run.

"I'm really sorry, Roux," he mumbled.

I flinched away from his hand that must have been making its way to my face. This was all too awkward! Why on earth did he have to stop me now, in front of all these prying eyes? We had never spoken outside of the bedroom or a club before. I really didn't want it to start happening now.

I wanted to ask what he was sorry for, it wasn't like he had done anything wrong. He wasn't the one who had shot me. His use of sorry in a pitiful way had my toes curling with annoyance. I just needed to get to my lecture!

"If I had known that-"

"There was no way for you to know, Zach," I said firmly. I could feel the eyes of the students burying into my back as harshly as Zach's were piercing my eyes. I was sure I would spontaneously combust from embarrassment at any moment. "Just drop it," I whispered harshly trying to move around him in the mass of students.

"But-"

"There's no need to be sorry for something you didn't do," I cut him off, while pushing past him towards my lecture room door. Zach's little stunt had all eyes on me. Whispers danced around the room like smoke, floating towards me before fizzling out. I tried to pay little attention to them, however, I felt my hands muddling and wringing together in front of me with anxiety.

I didn't look at anyone as I made my way into the large lecture hall. The room was brimming with students on a caffeine high, all ready to throw themselves into the lesson.

I trudged my way to the back of the classroom half-heartedly. I rarely sat back here, it had the worst view of the whiteboards up the front where I knew the professor would be writing. However, I was behind almost everyone else now. Unless they wanted to look like idiots and turn around to stare, I would be left alone for the most part.

The words from the professor seemed to drift in one ear and out of the other, as if there was nothing in my mind that could grasp onto the information. If I was being honest, I really didn't care what he was saying, instead choosing to take my time pulling out my laptop and sort through my thoughts. Usually I would have been on the edge of my seat, ensuring to encapsulate every sentence that fell from the professors' breath deep in my mind. This morning however, I wanted nothing more than to curl up in bed away from everyone and sleep.

"Declan Marcelo, everyone."

My heart was stuck throbbing in my throat with the professors words. There was no way. As I lifted my gaze, however, and peered down to the podium. There, in an expensive looking suit and tight man-bun, was Declan. His eyes wasted no time in roaming over the room, taking everyone in and seeming to be scanning their faces. I gave myself a mental pat on the back for sitting so far away.

What was he doing here? Surely this couldn't be to do with me, there was no way. If it wasn't though, why hadn't he mentioned coming to my lecture before? Maybe he didn't know it was mine, maybe I was overreacting. When his green eyes caught mine from the stage, however, my breath got stuck in my throat, the slow smile that came over his face held all the answers I needed.

"Good morning."

Gosh that voice. I was pretty sure he had captured the attention of almost everyone in the room who was into men with his simple greeting. His eyes stayed firmly on mine however, never wandering, his smile turning into a cunning smirk as my cheeks heated.

"As you all know, my name is Declan Marcelo, I am CEO of the Marcelo law firm in the inner city," he paused, looking around the room again. "I'm here to educate you all on an upcoming scholarship in which my firm has agreed to sponsor. We are aiming to choose the student who excels in your degree, someone who not only your professor but the English faculty speaks highly of, this scholarship is aimed to start at the beginning of next semester so those of you who are interested have plenty of time to catch up and prove yourselves. If you have any questions, your professor will happily answer them via email."

Just like that the room was buzzing with whispers and questions. Declan, however, didn't seem to mind as he made his way off of the podium and towards the chairs at the front of the room near the door. I had assumed he would leave, instead he plopped himself down rather ungracefully in one of the hard-plastic chairs and watched as the commotion in the room unfolded.

He sat throughout the whole class, eyes watching my every move as I ignored him. As the end of the lecture rolled around and the professor stopped talking, I wasted no time in shoving my things into my bag and skedaddling down the stairs to the door. I felt like I could finally breathe again.

A hand gripped my wrist as I tried to escape, pulling me back into the room. I spun around already knowing who was on the other end of the calloused hand holding me hostage.

"Let's go on a date."

My mouth hung open at his words.

CHAPTER 13

"What!" I exclaimed.

I tried to avoid the odd looks we received from the last few students trailing out the door.

"You mentioned on the phone that we hardly know each other, so let's fix that."

I couldn't believe this guy.

"I think you stalking my classes is telling me enough about you," I said sarcastically as I tried to walk around him.

I didn't miss the blush that formed on his cheeks as he stepped in my way.

"Miss Fallon, you're the one who turned down my scholarship, I need to find a new candidate so that it doesn't go to waste."

His words had my own blush flushing up my neck towards my face from embarrassment. I stepped around him again only to be blocked by his broad chest, a huff of annoyance fell from my lips.

"Roux."

I looked into his eyes and frowned.

"Why?" I asked. I had no idea why on earth he would

want to take me on a date. I had no interests in pursuing anything with this man and he needed to know that.

"Because I think if you saw things from my perspective you might rethink the dorm room situation. Just let me take you out for breakfast and we can talk-"

"I'm not interested in a relationship with anyone right now, Declan," I said abruptly, hoping he would understand that this was a definite no.

His familiar smirk peered back at me as I looked to meet his eyes.

"I never said anything about a relationship, Miss Fallon," he chuckled. "I should have been more clear on my definition of date, this is strictly business."

My face burnt with the heavy embarrassment that overcame me.

"I'm not accepting any of it."

The slow smile allowed for his sigh to fall out, almost as dramatically as Quinn's.

"Come on Roux," he cooed. "Let's talk about it."

This was a bad idea, a very bad one. Of course, a coffee was sure to help my frazzled brain and then I would be able to construct a more detailed sentence as to why he needed to listen to me.

"One coffee," I warned as I raised a finger. "And then you drop it."

"One coffee," he agreed.

"Off campus."

He merely smiled and rolled his eyes. The last thing I needed was for someone to see us together and come to conclusions. I could see the gossip now, *'Roux Fallon sleeps with Declan Marcelo for a scholarship.' No.* He dragged me towards the door.

"One more thing." I smiled.

He turned around with a curious look.

"You have to promise that I won't be the one you choose for the scholarship."

He smiled with me then.

"I'm not picking who it is at all, that's all up to the English department."

Shit. He dragged me out of the lecture room and down the hall.

I wasn't an idiot. I knew that I would be in the running for the scholarship. I had the grades and had made sure I had shown off my work ethic ever since I heard about the summer opportunity at Briggs Publishing. In order to be chosen for the program, I needed to be a top student, I never thought that my efforts would put me in such a bad situation.

I was pulled out of my thoughts when the sun hit my eyes and I squinted, realising we were headed outside. I snapped my arm back from Declan, ignoring his odd look. No one needed to know I knew him any better than they did. Not that I really did.

"So, where would you like to go for coffee?" Declan smirked as we neared the car park.

I knew where I wanted to go, Casper's. We couldn't do that though, it would be filled with students by this time of day.

"Anywhere not on campus."

He smiled before opening the fancy car door for me.

"Done."

The familiar leather seats were warm against my cold legs, the smoothness screaming luxury. Declan was in the car then, turning up the heaters and playing with the mirrors before we reversed out of the parking spot. I wasn't used to driving in silence, usually Quinn would have music blasting if we were to ever drive anywhere. Declan seemed to like it though, the awkward silence from our previous drive was engraved in my mind.

"So, Miss Fallon," he smirked. "Would you like to talk about why you can't accept my offer?"

Morals?

"I'm not accepting such an expensive upgrade or scholarship from someone I hardly know," I said honestly.

He seemed to be thinking about what I said for a moment before he nodded and smiled.

"Okay then, ask away."

"What?" I asked.

"Ask me anything you like, you said you hardly know me, let's fix that."

I was sure I was looking at him dumbfounded. Asking him questions wasn't going to change my answer. Knowing what his favourite colour was or the name of his first pet wasn't what I wanted out of this meeting.

"That's…" I really wasn't sure what to say. "I don't think that will help your case."

He smirked before rolling his eyes.

"You do realise you're debating with a lawyer, right?"

A blush crept to my cheeks and I quickly shook it away.

"I think you'll find me quite persistent."

"So am I," he replied while drumming his fingers on the wheel.

This guy, I thought, *this guy is going to be the death of me*. I had never met someone so elusive yet pungent in my whole life and I honestly wasn't sure if I ever wanted to again.

The buildings flew by as we drove down the familiar streets. I wasn't sure where we were going, but I knew that if he picked a café in the centre of the city we would have to park fifty billion blocks away and by the time we got there my legs would be aching. I hoped he was smart enough to think ahead.

"Well?" he asked, snapping my attention back to him. *Oh my gosh.* He really wasn't going to let this go. I rolled my eyes and shrugged my shoulders half-heartedly at his question. This was ridiculous.

"I'm not asking you some random questions in an effort for you to convince me to take your offer," I said sarcastically.

His eyebrows creased into the middle of his forehead as he frowned at me.

"Now that's a little rude, Miss Fallon," he joked. "Why don't I go first?"

Before I could open my mouth to protest he had already started.

"Why did you choose English as your major?"

Because it's the only thing I don't hate, I wanted to say.

"I enjoy it."

His grimace and eye roll had me holding back a smile.

"No one likes their major."

I couldn't help the smile that came over my face at his words.

"Well I do, I want to be a writer and I'm pretty sure in order to do that I'm going to have to enjoy writing. It's the only time of day that I look forward to," I joked. "Well, that and hanging out with Quinn and Will," I tried to add. I hadn't realised how utterly sad it had sounded. I promise I'm not crazy, I laughed to myself. *Oh gosh.* I probably shouldn't laugh with myself either.

I zoned back in as a smile overcame Declan's face.

"A writer, huh?" he mused. "I like it."

A blush took over my face, as I turned away. *Why did he have to be so ridiculous?*

CHAPTER 14

"And so basically, I ended up in the pool butt naked next to my professor."

The laugh bubbled uncontrollably from my lips as Declan finished telling his story.

"And that's why no one can enjoy their major," he finished, taking a slow sip of his cappuccino with a grin.

"That's the most ridiculous thing I've ever heard." I laughed, my stomach aching from the effort.

The other tables outside the coffee shop didn't feel any shame in staring at us I was sure. However, I was also positive that neither of us cared at this point. My coffee was long gone, being downed as quickly as it had arrived and I tried not to hate myself for staying just a little longer with him.

"So I want to know why you were so turned off going on a date with me," he grinned, eyebrows raised. "I must say you hurt my feelings," he said sarcastically, placing a hand on his chest.

"Spoken like a true male," I joked, rolling my eyes.

How on earth was I meant to explain my entire university life?

"There's a summer program," I started. "This publishing company chooses the top student from our university and others to participate and basically you're guaranteed to get published in the end."

I tried not to sound too serious, even though this was a topic I didn't joke about. Declan looked confused as he toyed with the napkin on the table.

"I've put in a lot of effort to make sure I have the best shot of being chosen and I'm not going to mess that up," I finished.

He eyed me over the rim of his cup. An eyebrow raised.

"So relationships are distractions for you?"

I wasn't sure why his question made me feel hot and embarrassed, although I knew I didn't like it.

"I guess," I mumbled, wishing I hadn't skulled my coffee, so that I had a distraction from his intense look. It wasn't any of his business anyway.

"So you're one of the top students in your class?" he asked.

I nodded, rolling my eyes at his question.

"If you're asking in regards to your scholarship, don't bother, I'll turn it down coming from your or the English department," I said seriously.

He only raised his hands and shook his head.

"I'm just curious," he said in a sarcastically polite voice.

Yeah right.

"Yes, I am."

His smirk only grew.

"Well, when you win that spot in the program and become a wildly successful author, you have to promise that I'll get the first signed copy." His smile was infectious and I soon found my eyes fluttering to the ground in an effort to not see his reaction to my beet red cheeks.

"I think you'll have to fight my mother for that one," I muttered.

His chuckle had my stomach clenching and before I realised it I was sitting straighter in my seat. Eyes on my empty coffee mug and shoulders back. I shouldn't have been here laughing with this man over something that would definitely not be in the foreseeable future, if I let myself get distracted by him. I had made sure that my distractions were chosen accordingly over the years, like Zach, who had agreed that we were nothing more than fun. And the joking mannerisms that Declan was flourishing with were something that I wasn't going to allow myself to get used to them. I had to focus on my work, on my study and perfecting my assignments. Not on what to say to make Declan Marcelo laugh. I had put too much effort in getting where I was, I wasn't quitting now.

"Well, my coffee is finished." I smiled politely. "And I don't think I have really heard a word about the dorm come out of your mouth, which, mind you, I am very thankful for, however, it probably means that it's not the biggest deal on your mind right now." I smiled. "So thank you very much for the coffee, Mr Marcelo. I should probably be getting back to campus to sort this all out."

"Do you enjoy life with no distractions, Miss Fallon?"

His question had me stop in my tracks, my book bag slung half-heartedly over my shoulder, slowly slipping down. *How was someone meant to answer that? Where did that even come from?* Why did he still look so freaking casual? With his 'stare-into-your-mother-fucking-soul' eyes.

"Yes," I said blandly as I pulled up my book bag and straightened out my pants. "And I'll enjoy it a lot more when I'm published."

His smile made it seem like he knew something I didn't,

as if he could see into the future and found something he saw funny. I didn't like it.

"Well then, I guess I better get you home," he murmured, standing from his seat and quickly knocking back the last of what I was sure had to be, a cold coffee.

"You really don't have to."

The last thing I wanted right now was him to spring some more, insightful I'm-a-man-and-therefore-im-a-brooding-hunk bullshit on me again.

"Roux," he said softly, smiling as his hand gently sat on my lower back. "Let's go."

The warmth from his hand, pressed its way through the fabric of my coat and had my protests turning to mush in my mouth. The heated seats in his car sure seemed better than the heaters in a taxi, so my mouth remained shut as he led me around the corner to the parking spot which had oddly enough been left open. I didn't want to know whether or not it had been dumb luck.

I wasn't sure if I would ever get used to him opening the car door for me, or the warmth of his heated leather seats and yet upon having these thoughts I needed to remind myself that I wouldn't have to get used to it, if I had anything to say about it.

As the car roared to life I couldn't help but look at him with the most pleading eyes I could muster.

"Can we please, for the love of God, turn on the radio?"

His burst of loud laughter had me jumping in my seat as his head was thrown back, a belly tickling laugh rumbling in the car. I could tell his eyes were watering and his breathing was short and sharp as he continued giggling like a child, one hand gripping the steering wheel for dear life and the other pressing the screen.

"On one condition," he mused, still shaking with whatever the hell he found so funny about all of this. I was sure I wasn't going to like his offer. "I get to distract you for one whole afternoon."

My stomach dropped. He couldn't possibly mean what I thought he had meant. There was no way.

"What?"

"Distractions can be a good thing Miss Fallon, and I don't think that you have gotten to know me well enough to make your decision yet. Let me distract you for a full afternoon, doing whatever I plan and I'll even let you choose the station," he chuckled.

Was he? No. No. He couldn't possibly be asking what I thought he was. I half jumped out of my skin, when some form of heavy metal music started blasting throughout the car. This only made Declan laugh harder.

"Well, the music's playing now so I guess you don't have a choice but to agree," he all but shouted over the music. It rang so hard in my ears that I was sure I was going to barf up guitar strings, making my mind whirl and jumbled and it was so freaking loud!

"Fine!" I called over the music. "Just, please switch it!"

The music seemed to automatically switch to a soft pop song and my head hummed. I wasn't sure why I was breathing so intensely, it wasn't as if the music had caused me to exercise in any way, however, as I gripped the door for dear life and slowly let my shoulders fall, I was sure I sounded like I had run a marathon.

"Was that really necessary?" I asked quietly, as my head fell into my hands.

His smooth voice came back quickly with his cunning reply.

"I told you, Miss Fallon, you're arguing with a lawyer."

Yeah, a bloody childish one.

CHAPTER 15

The tapping of my pen on my textbook was annoying me, and yet as my mind raced I couldn't bring myself to stop. My test was on Friday, Friday! I had two days to study for this bloody thing and I had absolutely no idea what I was even meant to be revising.

My day had turned even more sour earlier that morning when Hannah had asked me to join their study group this afternoon. I felt terrible saying no, however, after what happened last time, soothing in my stomach was warning me that it might not be the best idea, even after she offered to walk with me. I didn't want this to be a "thing" though. I didn't want to be that girl who was always so scared to go out walking or jogging by themselves. Not that the jogging part happened frequently. I just hoped that they bought my lie about my mother coming to visit and that they didn't think I was being a pansy because of what happened.

The thoughts of my mother made me wonder how long it had really been since I had spoken to her. *Probably not that long,* I reassured myself. Long enough though, that I was sure to expect a call from her within the next few days. She hadn't visited this month and I was sure it was weighing down on her. Even my chest felt heavy from the lack of contact, I was sure for my mother it was worse. She seemed to miss me, even when we were together.

Still, the guilt ate away at me for the hours I tried to wrap my brain around my study notes. I really should have taken up the offer for extra help studying. I knew this test wasn't going to be a piece of cake but more like a sour slice of lemon meringue pie. *Oh gosh,* now I was making myself hungry. Even my stomach wasn't enjoying our new dorm room. The distance from Quinn meant that I ate most of my meals alone and I wasn't used to only having myself for company. I really needed to go and speak with the chairman again, or even the university committee, whoever I needed to so that this was all sorted with quick and easy.

Why oh why did life have to get so complicated? I needed Quinn, I needed her dramatics and antics to help distract me from life enough that I could focus on my studies. As ironic as that sounded.

'*Studying, come help?*'

Her reply came almost instantly.

'*Oh thank God, we gotta talk! Be there in 5 xx.*'

I had barely resumed my studying when I heard quick footsteps in the hall outside. The short knock on the door had my eyebrows drawing and a frown overtaking my face. Quinn couldn't have gotten here that fast...

Slowly, I moved my way from the lounge, my eyes never leaving the door as I made my way to it sceptically. However, as I peered through the eyehole, I could make out Quinn's frantic face as she bopped up and down on her heels. *What the heck?*

She must have heard the lock, because as soon as it was openable, I was nearly being slapped by the back of the door. She didn't seem to care though, as she marched her way past me, throwing her bag quite literally onto the ground and huffing all about.

"How?" was all I asked as I marvelled at her in amazement. It took me half an hour to walk to her dorm from here. She looked at me as if I had grown a third head for a moment before her mouth dropped open and she smiled breathlessly.

"I was at Will's." She laughed, making her way to the lounge and flopping down like a pancake. "I know we were gonna study but girl," she drew in some more breaths as she paused. The look on her face was pure insanity as she eyed me with wide eyes. "I think he almost kissed me."

"What?" Holy cow! "Oh my gosh!"

"I know!" she screamed, her face already turning back to the shade of red, it was when she arrived. "We were sitting on the lounge and talking about the end of year showcase and I said I needed to find a date for the dinner afterwards and he said maybe one of the theatre guys would want to take me but I said I didn't want one of the theatre guys and he asked who I wanted to take and I said if he was free I wanted to go with him and he started leaning in and oh my gosh!" She drew in a giant breath.

Finally! I wanted to scream, I wanted to cry! My ship was actually sailing! *Oh my gosh* and I thought today was going to be unproductive!

"And then you messaged and I think we both freaked out but oh my gosh Roux, it nearly happened!"

My pursed lips were no doubt holding back the scream that I wanted to release. I had set fire to the ship! Paused it and allowed it to go on hold even longer than it already had been! *Damn it Roux!*

"No, I'm glad it didn't happen like that!" Quinn assured, no doubt seeing my seething look. "I want it to be so much better than the rushed mess it would have been if it had happened then." She smiled at me, her arms joggling about. "But oh my gosh," she whispered.

I wasn't sure who was more excited as my heart raced in my chest. I felt like I was on top of the world! Finally!

"Well, then what are you doing here? Go get your man!"

She shook her head quickly, eyeing me as if I was crazy.

"I can't go back now! And eww, don't call Will my man. I need to decongest my brain from a crazy town before I can bring myself to go talk to him! I can't mess this up! What if it wasn't even going to end like that?"

I held back the inevitable eye-roll for a second before I caved.

"You're an idiot."

"I'm not an idiot," she defended. "I simply value our friendship enough to only move forward when I know that it's actually in the cards."

"It is in the cards," I said blandly. She just nodded her head with a sarcastic look. She could deny it all she wanted, but they were the ones in the way of their ever-pending relationship.

"Well Declan asked me on a date, so I guess we're both doing well in that department."

Her head spun around so fast I was scared it was going to roll off of her shoulders.

"What?" she screamed, jumping from the lounge with a grin. "When, how? Oh my gosh you said yes, right?"

"I didn't say anything. You know I don't do dates."

She was a fish out of water, opening and snapping shut her mouth so much, I feared her jaw would fall off.

"ROUX!"

"Quinn!" I mimicked, smiling.

"You literally saved this guy's life and now he's a wildly successful lawyer, I think you should give this a go," she said sarcastically.

"You're forgetting the part where he is practically forcing me to accept his dorm room and pressuring me into a scholarship. I'm pretty sure the only reason he wants to go is so that he can convince me to accept."

"Now who's the idiot?" she fired back dramatically, her hands being thrown all about to try and get her point across. "I wish I was in your position!" She laughed.

"It's complicated."

"Mhmm," her eye-roll didn't go unnoticed. "Complicated my ass!"

"Quinn-"

The sound of my ringtone had me stopping abruptly. What was even worse was the name that flashed across the screen as I pulled it out of my pocket. Declan. This ought to be good. I hit the power button and watched as it turned off. There was no way I was going to answer that in front of Quinn.

"Who was...oh my gosh, that was him, wasn't it?"

Shit.

"It was my mum Quinn," I lied.

"Bullshit!" She laughed, jumping about excitedly. "Call him back!" she squealed.

"No."

"Yes!"

"Quinn," I warned softly. I didn't want to go on a date with him. The coffee had been tense enough.

"Oh come on, Roux!" she burst. "You never do anything fun! Just this once, can't you go with your gut and not that fancy brain of yours? What's the worst that can happen? He only wanted you to go so that he could convince you to take his offer? So what? Just say no! Think about the positives! This guy could really like you!"

As if!

"He doesn't know me well enough to like me, Quinn."

"That's the point of a date," she groaned. "Come on, Roux!"

"I'll tell you what," I said annoyed. "I'll go on a date with Declan the day that you tell William how you really feel, the use of the word love and everything."

I could see this was a pill she found hard to swallow. Confusion and annoyance flooding her features.

"Roux," she murmured lowly. "That's not fair."

"Yes it is!" I laughed humourlessly. "If you want to have such a big say in my love life, then I'm going to do the same. You and Will have been teetering on the edge of the dating pool for too long! You both clearly like each other otherwise none of this would be happening! Go and talk to him Quinn and I'll do the same, if I have to put on my big girl pants then you're chucking on a pair as well," I huffed.

"You know what? Fine, fine! If you think you're so clever, I'll message him right now and when I get horribly rejected and my heart breaks, it'll be your fault!" she yelled dramatically.

"Just do it, Quinn!"

"Fine!"

She had her phone in her hands in a matter of seconds, her fingers moving so quickly over the keys that I was scared she would make a typo and ruin the sentimental moment. I wasted no time in jumping over to read what she was typing.

Will, I think we need to talk, really talk about all of this. I do want you to be my date but-

She paused.

"Why'd you stop?" I groaned, frantically looking from the phone to her.

"Shush, this is my moment!"

It's obvious we're not just friends, we never were. I think I liked you even when you wore those hideous purple gumboots to kinder-

garten and I think I more than liked you when we decided to go to the end of year dance in year seven. I think in all honesty. Truly.

She took a big breath in, eyes going wide as she eyed the screen.

I might even love you.

Her fingers were moving so fast she didn't even seem to blink before she hit the send button. Her face turned red and she threw her phone on the lounge, groaning.

"There! Happy now?" She asked, grimacing before covering her face with her hands.

"Yes." I smiled. Finally, finally I would have to third wheel a friendship and could just third wheel a relationship. She eyed me Then her face dropped. Her eyes grew wide and it looked as if she had stopped breathing.

"Oh my fucking God, Roux. What did I just do? No. No!" She lunged for her phone at the same time I lounged for her. Her fingers barely skimmed the lounge before she was plummeted to the ground, me straddling her.

"No way, Quinny!" I yelled happily. "It's happening!"

"No!" She struggled.

The dinging of her phone had me going giddy with happiness.

"Yes!" I screamed. I sure hoped these walls were soundproof and that Will wasn't downstairs listening to our pow wow moment.

I let her go as she scrambled over to her phone with wide eyes. She was still for a moment, looking at her phone as if it was going to blow up in her hand before she slowly allowed her eyes to meet mine.

"Well?" I asked excitedly.

A grin broke over her face.

"He said to come back over so that he can ask me out on a date properly," she whispered. "Oh my God!" She screamed, jumping up and spinning around doing some form of a weird jig. "I'm sorry, Roux I-"

"Don't be sorry! Go!" I laughed.

She joined in, grabbing her jacket off the lounge and throwing her arms around me quickly before she ran to the door. She opened it quickly, spinning around on her feet to give me a sarcastic glare.

"Call him back," she said sternly, before squealing again and running out the door, slamming it behind her.

Shit. I forgot about that part.

As I looked down at my phone, still riding the waves of Quinn's high, I shrugged. May as well get it over with.

CHAPTER 16

I was sure I was meant to feel nervous, maybe a little excited but certainly not the cool all and connectedness that I was feeling at that moment. Declan was going to be here any second and I felt nothing other than curiosity as to where we were going. He wouldn't tell me on the phone when I had called to ask and accept his invitation, simply stating that I would have to wait and see. If I was being honest, I was just looking forward to getting away from campus for a while.

My life had been seeming to revolve around studying even more than usual lately, I would be lying if I said it didn't have something to do with me being a little nervous to visit Caspers, or go for a walk on my own. There was only so much free time that Quinn had. My test had been absolutely brutal and I could only imagine what my score would be.

Seeing as how I had no idea where I was being taken, I had dressed casually. My pants and blouse seemed fitting for the warmer day, however I had slung a jacket over my shoulder just in case. As a short knock sounded behind the door, I sighed and made my way to open it, ignoring the string of messages I was sure were coming from Quinn, wondering how everything was going.

However, as I opened the door, I was taken aback by the large toque of flowers that appeared in front of my face.

"Good morning," Declan greeted enthusiastically as he held them out to me. I took them with wide eyes. I most certainly hadn't been expecting these.

"Good morning," I mumbled awkwardly, taking the flowers to the kitchen. "What are these for?" I asked as I filled a vase.

It was as he was rocking back and forth on his heels that I realised how more casual his outfit was today in comparison to the suit he had worn before. His jeans and hoodie almost made him seem like a completely different person and I secretly laughed inside. It was odd seeing him so casual.

"I figured your old ones would have died by now," he shrugged, leaning against the breakfast bar smirking.

They had. I simply nodded and moved them to the table, where the others had sat just days before. I had never been one to buy and keep flowers in the house, however, it seemed to make the room smell nice, so I wasn't complaining about Declan's antics.

"Are you ready to go?" he asked, eyebrows raised as he motioned for the door.

"Yep," I shrugged, making sure to shove my phone and keys in my pocket.

He trailed behind as we made our way down the hallway and stairs, which I had come to not mind. I was glad that most students had slept in on Saturday mornings.

The last thing I wanted was for people to stare and come up with their own conclusions as to what was happening. Even though we were technically going on some form of a date. They didn't need to know that.

I found myself quickly shuffling into my jacket as we

walked out of the glass doors to the carpark, the air outside much colder than it had been in my dorm building. We wasted no time in walking over to his sleek car, avoiding the puddles on the road. He approached me briskly as I waited for him to unlock the car. I tired no to look confused as he got closer. The heat radiated off from him, as he bent down to my level, my breath catching in my throat as his face appeared in front of my own.

However, as he opened my door and my face flushed, I quickly scampered into the car to escape his satisfied smile and knowing eyes. *Asshole.* It only took some deep breaths before I felt the flush die down. I still avoided his gaze as he opened his door and got into the car though, the last thing I needed was to think that he was affecting me in any way. Especially when I wanted to talk about finally getting back to my old dorm room and being closer with Quinn. I was missing our movie nights and hating the distance in between our buildings.

I tried not to smile as he reached over and flicked on the radio, allowing the silence to be taken over by a familiar pop song. I swallowed, looking over at his clean-shaven face.

"So where are we going?"

"As if I'm going to tell you," he joked, as we pulled out of the campus.

I made sure he saw my exaggerated eye-roll, his laughter blending in with the music.

"It's somewhere I think you will like." He smiled, turning away from the main roads and down a small street.

The buildings here looked older and more run down than any the main city had to offer, most here seemed to be turned into apartment buildings or cafés. I hadn't been to the slower parts of the city in yonks, I wasn't sure if I had ever been down this street. I tended to avoid places with a low population and after what happened the other day I was thinking it was a good idea. Of course, it was a little hard to feel stressed about such things, with a six foot-something mammoth in the car beside me. I instead focused on the lake outside the window, which seemed less affected in this part of town, one might say even beautiful in the morning light.

The car slowed to a stop outside of a small and tidy looking building. Declan wasted no time in jumping out of the car and rushed around to my side. I tried my hardest to get my seatbelt unbuckled and open the door before he did, however, I missed my opportunity by a mere second. Dejectedly, pulled myself out of the car and frowned at my loss, even if Declan didn't know it was a competition.

We weren't so far out of the city scene that we couldn't see the buildings, the small suburb vibes that the area was giving off reminded me more of my hometown than any other part of the city had. I couldn't help but smile at the comfort it brought.

The door to the building was old and worn down, yet somehow it still managed to look clean in a vintage way. It didn't creak when Declan opened it, the only noise being the chime of a bell signalling that we had entered. However, as I turned to look at the rest of the room, a small gasp escaped my mouth at what I saw. Books and plants scattered the inside of the room on shelves and tables everywhere. A bookshop.

An old man arose from behind a vintage looking desk, eyeing us with a contagious smile.

"Well, look what the wind blew in," he cheered, wobbling over to us as fast as his legs would allow him. "It's good to see you again, little Marcelo." He smiled, holding out his hand for Declan to shake. I tried not to seem as surprised as I felt, when Declan pulled the fragile man in for a hug instead.

"You know how I feel about that name Mr Jones," he

joked as he pulled away. The old man simply waved him off and turned to me.

"And who might this pretty lady be?" he asked, eyes darting between Declan and myself.

"Roux," Declan stated simply, eyes catching mine before turning back to Mr Jones. "We're just here to pick out some books," he added in an unhelpful manner.

"Of course, of course!" Mr Jones hurried, hurrying himself out of our way. "I'll be waiting at the registers with a trailer," he seemed to joke, laughing at himself whilst Declan shook his head.

I hadn't picked him as a book type of person, of course as he expertly dragged me through the aisles to where he wanted to go it was obvious that I was wrong.

I couldn't help but look in awe at the pristine books sitting on the old vintage shelves. It was a beautifully put together store, with plants seeming to take over the back corner, branching out throughout the space and popping up from nowhere.

"I figured you would like books." Declan laughed. "Considering," he gestured at myself.

He had stopped us in the classics section of the store, and I tried not to smirk.

"Did I get your favourite genre right at least?" he asked, seeming happy with himself. I tried not to scrunch up my nose too much as I eyed the books, shaking my head and smiling. I quickly grabbed his hand and dragged him back to where I had seen the romance section.

"When you're constantly having to annotate classics, I don't think you can really get into them that much," I explained as he pouted jokingly. "But," I paused as I looked at the books around me. "I never grew out of my love for cliches."

I could see him eyeing the titles before he looked at me with a frown.

"You have got to be kidding me." He laughed.

"What?" I asked, crossing my arms over my chest jokingly.

He looked at me as if I had grown a second head.

"I just expected more from an English major," he mumbled with a smirk.

I gaped at him in offence and picked up a random book from the shelf, ignoring his soft chuckles.

"For all you know this could be great," I said sternly, motioning to the book in my hand.

The belly rumbling laughter that fell from his lips as he looked at the book had my own stomach tightening.

"I mean it's not impossible," he said, motioning to the book.

I looked down at the book and blushed. The very poorly designed cover seemed ridiculously un-great, however, I clutched it to my chest regardless, looking up at him with as much dignity as I could muster.

"Well, I'm going to get it," I said, turning around and grimacing at the thought of actually having to get the book. I hand made it a step though, when the book was quickly plucked from my arm. I turned around, shocked, staring at a smirking Declan, who now held my book.

"I invited you on this date so I'm paying," he said, smiling cheekily down at me.

"No."

He simply rolled his eyes and moved on to browse the titles ahead.

"Yes, Miss Fallon," he mumbled. "You can invite me on the next date and I'll let you pay."

I paused, smirking.

"So this is a date?" I asked cheekily. Obviously, it was. However, Declan was still yet to call it as such.

He paused ahead of me, turning slowly with a glint in his eyes.

"Well, that depends, Miss Fallon, do you admit that I'm a fairly good distraction?" he asked.

I found my face flaring as I remember our last 'date'.

"Perhaps," I answered sarcastically.

He smiled before looking at the floor to his shoes.

"Then I guess it is."

I clamped my mouth shut at his words and turned back to the shelf of books. I was not going there right now. I guess it didn't matter that much if he paid anyway, if I didn't pick an unreasonable amount of books, then he wouldn't need to spend too much.

I wasn't sure how long I spent browsing over the titles of books, pulling a few out before shoving them back in. I was not picking a book unless I thought I absolutely wouldn't be able to stop thinking about it if I didn't get it. Not when Declan had made it clear that he was paying.

"So how did you come across this place?" I asked Declan, as I bent down to look at the lower shelves.

"It was my father's first business."

My eyes almost bulged out of my face as I tried to keep my reaction hidden. I wasn't expecting to be taken somewhere so serious.

"Oh," I mumbled softly, still eyeing the books in front of me.

"He used the money from selling this store to open his first publishing company in the city," he continued. "It's no longer under the Marcelo name though, he sold it a long time ago, it's now Briggs publishing."

I swung around quickly as I registered what he had said. Briggs Publishing was possibly the largest publishing company in the country. It was also the company in which I was trying to be chosen for their summer program.

"What?" I choked out. Then I noticed the huge stack of books in his arms. "Whoa," I mumbled.

Looking closer however, I realised most of them were titles that I had been looking at.

"Declan!"

He attempted to wave me off as I eyed the pile, pushing past me clumsily with all the books. I reached up to grab half, ready to shove them back on the shelf, however, his whine stopped me.

"Roux," he drew out.

"No," I said as I stuffed them back in their slots.

Sitting the stack on the floor, I tried to stop him as he tried behind me, pulling the books out from where I was putting them.

"Declan!" I grumbled.

His eye-roll almost outdid mine as he huffed.

"All great writers must first be great readers, Roux."

"And who said that?" I asked sarcastically, rolling my eyes as my hands found my hips.

"My father," he answered.

The look he gave was challenging and I found myself giving up and throwing my head back.

"I do not need all of these books, Declan," I groaned.

Satisfied he began picking up the books from the floor.

"Yes, but I really don't care." He smiled.

I sighed in defeat behind him as we made our way to the counter.

CHAPTER 17

Declan had thought that we hadn't spent enough time at the bookshop, instead he dragged me to another café in the area stating that the whole point was to get to know each other better and he still hardly knew anything about me. We both knew what this really was leading to though, him trying to convince me to keep the dorm room, I had hoped he had given up on the scholarship by now and that by some miracle the English department chose someone else. Even if I could turn down the offer after they had chosen me, I didn't want to be stuck in another situation with this. I wanted it over with.

He sat across from me outside the small café, the large stack of books had been left behind, laid carefully in the backseat of his car. I had been quicker than him at the register here, however, and was able to pay for both of our coffees.

"I didn't pick you as the coffee drinker," he mused, as I chugged down my black coffee.

Bewildered, I gaped at him as he sipped his cappuccino.

"Well, you are very mistaken," I said dramatically.

He laughed, looking down at my cup, which was almost empty.

"It does seem so."

The silence had me thinking about something to say.

"So why didn't you go into the family business?" I asked.

He looked at me as if I had set his dog on fire, almost sitting out his coffee.

"I was always better at speaking compared to writing," he said after coughing up the rest of his drink.

I nodded as I recalled his talk in the classroom. He was a demanding speaker, I assumed this would be good in his profession.

"Of course my father did pass down the love for reading." He smirked.

I couldn't picture him sitting down and reading a book, to me he seemed more like the type to be lifting weights in the gym. My eyebrow raised in question at his words. It was obvious from the bookstore that he was telling the truth but I couldn't believe someone like Declan would actually have the patience to read.

He responded to my expression with faux hurt, placing a hand over his chest sarcastically as if I had wounded his feelings.

"Are you underestimating my intelligence, Miss Fallon?" he asked.

"Of course not, Mr Marcelo," I joked.

He watched me for a moment as I downed the rest of my coffee, his eyes strained on mine.

"We should probably get you home soon," he mumbled, looking down to the table and clearing his throat. "The sky is looking a little grey."

The sky did look like it was about to pour down rain. I didn't have time to get a cold.

"Okay," I nodded, knocking back the rest of my drink.

Declan seemed tense as we walked along the footpath to the car, eyeing the men at the corner of the street oddly. I couldn't help but tense myself, when I realised that the men were staring back quite intensely. I couldn't help but look up at Declan as we passed them, assuring myself that nothing would happen so long as he was here, no matter how scary the group of men looked.

However, as we passed them and their eyes moved on to stare at the birds chirping prettily throughout the trees, I wanted to scold myself for being so judgmental. I probably would have stared at Declan and myself as well. We looked like a bit of an odd mix.

As we neared the car, Declan seemed to have relaxed. His casual demeanour back as he opened the door and gave me a slight smile. He wasted no time in slipping in himself, turning the radio onto a comfortable volume and bopping his head along to the music. I didn't feel the need to fill the space with small talk, instead opting to rest my head against the seat and watch the buildings fly by.

By the time we had reached my dorm room door, the silence had enveloped us completely and I felt bad for breaking it by laughing at Declan, who looked like he was going to topple over with the large stack of books he was carrying. Thankfully, not all had been for me, apparently 'not all books in the romance section looked as bad as the one I picked'. The butt-crack. He seemed to manage just fine with the large stack though, piling them onto the dining table and smiling at his efforts happily.

"I had a lot of fun today, Roux." He grinned. I hadn't expected him to want to leave so soon, nor had I been prepared to want him to stay. Despite my best efforts to get away from him, today was good. Great, actually. Possibly one of the best days I have had in a while and I was glad that I had accepted to go on the date, even if a word about the dorm hadn't been mentioned…yet.

"Me too," I smiled up at him, shuffling my feet on the wooden floor. It had been the first point in the day in which I had felt awkward and I tried to brush it off.

"I should, you know," he fumbled over his words as he scratched his neck, pointing at the door.

"Or you could stay?"

His head bobbed up and down quickly as his grin turned into a chuckle as he grabbed a book from the stack.

"We could read?" he offered, shrugging as if it wasn't the weirdest thing to do on a date ever. His face fell as he looked down at the book that he held in his hands, having picked up the novel in which he earlier thought wouldn't be any good, frowning, he handed me the book.

"If you think it will be so great," he teased. I rolled my eyes, sitting my phone on the table, which hadn't stopped buzzing since I got back to my dorm room, probably having William looking out his window to see when we arrived, like a spy.

I turned back around to see him stretching out over the lounge, a new book in hand as he got comfortable. I followed suit, frowning at the book in my hands. Stupid pride. I tried to sit in between Declan's legs, his whole body now spread across my lounge as if it were a bed. Oddly enough, it was comfortable and I settled into the back of the lounge, looking down at Declan who had already begun reading.

My breath quickened as I felt one of his hands come to rest on my thigh, slowly rubbing gentle patterns as he read. I tried to focus on the words in front of me and not on the warm fingers tracing circles on my leg. The soft movements made it hard to concentrate, my eyes growing heavy and tired, whilst my mind was the most awake it had been all day.

The breeze outside flew in from the window, cooling my

hot face and helping me turn each page, if I wasn't concentrating so hard on not focusing on Declan, I may have even fallen asleep. I hoped he wouldn't mind, as I spun around to rest my head on his chest, my neck aching from standing stiff whilst I read. He didn't seem to have any complaints as his hands moved to my hair. This time I allowed my eyes to flutter, closed if just for a second, to relish in the feeling of his hand massaging against my head. Best. Date. Ever.

I allowed myself to enjoy it for a moment longer, my body seeming to somehow find a state of relaxation in its overthinking state. I wasn't sure why he was doing it, as I looked up, however, he was still, nose deep in his book. I wasn't sure if he even realised his hands were still tangled. I opted to resume my reading, and not think about it.

I wasn't sure how long I had been reading for when Declan shuffled underneath me, the book in my hands having exceeded all expectations and possibly being quite good.

"It's getting a little late," he mumbled as he sat the book down on the table, stretching his arms above his head.

My eyes drifted to the window which now showed the setting sun. I had wasted so much time today, yet I didn't seem to care.

"Im sorry," I mumbled, sitting up quickly. "I didn't realise."

I heard a soft chuckle before his hands gently wrapped around my waist to spin me around. Once I was facing him and his soft smile he shook his head.

"Please don't be sorry," he murmured, looking down at me happily. "Today was so much better than I thought it would be," he chuckled softly.

I knew how he felt. I hadn't expected to enjoy myself today, yet here I was, feeling giddy at the sight of someone whom days ago I disliked.

"Thank you, for today," I whispered, staring up at him.

His eyes never left mine as his hand came to rest on my cheek, a knowing look coming over his eyes as he sighed.

"There's one flaw in that favourite genre of yours," he mumbled, thumb running over my jaw.

"What?" I breathed out as his face grew closer.

"The real thing is so much better."

Then his lips were on mine. I couldn't breathe. I couldn't think. He was kissing me, his hands cupping my cheeks as I felt him smile against my lips. They were softer than I'd imagined, gentle and sweet as he slowly pulled back, quicker than I wanted. I was sure my cheeks were red.

"I better get going." He smiled, his lips pressing against my forehead. "I'd like to do this again."

"Me too," I whispered as he pulled back. I didn't want him to go.

As I walked him to the door, he turned slowly before he left, giving me that cheeky grin.

"I'll call you."

"You better," I joked.

He chuckled as he took a step back, and I watched him slowly walk down the hallway.

What a fucking day.

CHAPTER 18

I closed the door and waited for a single moment, before I allowed myself to let out the uncontrollable giggles I had been holding in all day. *Why, oh why did today have to go well?* I felt tired in a good way, my body begging to go back into the state of relaxation it had been in moments before. There was no point in going to sleep now though. No. I still needed to call Quinn and have a deep dive into what the heck just went down.

Her messages were endless as I opened my phone, however, I ignored them and clicked the dial button instead.

"Rouxette Fallon!" she screeched from the other end of the line before laughing. "Well, it couldn't have gone too badly! You haven't messaged me back all day!"

"We need to talk!" I laughed excitedly. Her squeal on the other end only fuelled my happiness.

"Yes! Ugh I'm so excited! Finally some real goss! Can you meet me in my dorm in 30?" she asked.

"Yes!"

She hung up. *Oh my gosh.* What on earth had I gotten myself into? I didn't waste time thinking about the ways in which today might cause issues, I threw on my coat, grabbed my phone and book bag and basically ran to Quinn's. I wanted to tell her everything about today, although I also knew I would feel guilty for not doing anything all day, hopefully my book bag had everything I needed in it to get a little bit done while I dished out the goods.

As I quickly made my way to her dorm, I realised the sun had yet to set completely and I couldn't help but feel relieved for the extra light along the way. The last thing I wanted was to walk the path in the dark. I'm sure I would freak myself out before I ever got to Quinn's. The path also, was luckily filled with a few stray students here and there, I hardly had to be cautious at all.

My familiar dorm building looked the same and I felt sad with the waves of nostalgia that washed over me. I had been in the same building on the same floor as Quinn since we started three years ago. The familiar stairs and broken elevator lead me up to my floor. I even almost turned down the right hallway instead of the left, to my old dorm room. As I did, however, my door caught my eye and my mouth dropped open. The yellow tape on the door looked like it had been carelessly taped everywhere over the chipped wooden door. Which hung slightly ajar in the door frame.

Quinn opened her door after my third frantic knock, eyeing me with a smile before she saw my face.

"What happened to my door?" I asked quickly.

She smirked while stepping aside for me to come in.

"Well, if you bothered to message your bestest friend back you might have known."

"Sorry," I smiled sheepishly.

"No you're not," she rolled her eyes, "But I wouldn't be either. They think there was a break in last night."

"A break in? What!"

She rolled her eyes and dragged me over to the bed before shoving me down on it.

"Don't worry, probably just a junkie that realised it was free."

"That's not helping," I laughed at her, before my eyes widened. "What am I meant to do about the dorm room then? I've been trying to get transferred back," I asked. She rolled her eyes and shrugged.

"Enjoy the new villa you have?"

Frowning, I ignored her. I still couldn't accept it permanently.

"Oh you so did not bring study stuff!" She whined, eyeing the book bag sling over my shoulder. I smiled at her, wiggling my eyebrows.

"Oh yes, I did."

She groaned, throwing herself back dramatically on the bed.

"I need to catch up!" I defended, getting comfortable beside her.

"So do I," she sassed, "on your date!"

I couldn't help but laugh at her demands as I threw my book-bag onto the bed.

"I can multitask."

"So what happened?" she asked. "I want every detail!"

I had never pictured myself to be sitting on Quinn's bed telling her about a date that I, Roux Fallon, had gone on.

"Well, he showed up at my door early this morning with flowers," she nodded enthusiastically, drawing the bed cover up to her chin. "Then we went to a bookstore and oh my gosh Quinn this bookstore, it was like paradise!" I smiled giddily at the thought. "Then he wouldn't let me buy any books, oh my gosh Quinn the amount of books he picked! And it turns out it was his father's store, well, not anymore but that's beside the point, then we went for coffee and he was hilarious! And then when he took me home I asked him to stay and-"

"Oh my gosh did you guys do it?" she screeched, excitedly bouncing up and down on the bed.

"What! No!" I defended annoyed. "But we did read and he ran his fingers through my hair and oh my gosh Quinn, it was the best feeling ever and it was just the most casual chill date ever and it was great," I finished stupidly. I knew I had sounded like a child on a sugar high but I couldn't help it. It had been a really good day.

"Ahhh!" she squealed, fist pumping the air.

"I'm so happy! My baby is all growing up!"

Rolling my eyes at her, I ran my hands over my smiling face.

She opened her mouth at the same time the knock at the door had us both jumping. Quinn looked at it curiously, seeming to not be expecting anyone. She tilted to the door cautiously and peeped through the hole.

"No way," she whispered groaned, throwing her hands cup in the air.

I looked at her confused before she rolled her eyes, opening the door to reveal a frazzled looking Zach. *Oh.*

"Quinn! I'm sorry but I went to Roux's room and-"

"Hey Zach," I said plainly, moving to the other end of the bed so that he could see me.

His eyes went wide and it looked as if he was contemplating pushing past Quinn.

"Roux! Oh my God, are you okay?" he asked, motioning down the hall, where I'm guessing he saw my door.

"Yeah," I said tiredly. I really didn't want to get into this right now.

"What happened?" he asked, eyeing me confused.

I wasn't sure whether or not to tell him that I had actually moved dorms, as much as I didn't mind Zach, I knew what he would have been going to my dorm for in the first place and I didn't feel like having a discussion about that right now.

"Break in, don't worry I wasn't there."

Quinn eyed me knowingly as she nodded her head.

"I'm so sorry," he said sincerely.

"That's all good Zach, it wasn't your fault. Thanks for coming and checking in on me though," I said politely, hoping he took the hint to leave.

He only nodded his head at me once and slowly stepped back from the door with a frown. Quinn pushed it shut, and as soon as I heard it click I groaned, throwing myself back onto the bed. I knew I had to address the Zach situation sooner rather than later. I couldn't see him again, not when I was so wrapped up in a single date with Declan.

"Girl," Quinn sighed as she came to sit on the bed.

"I know," I groaned as I opened my book bag.

CHAPTER 19

I hadn't thought through to the lonely walk I had back to my dorm room. It was dark now, the pizza we had ordered rumbling in an uncomfortable way with anxiousness. I was glad that the lights along the path were still lit and the path between buildings was so close to the main section of the campus. Surely, nothing could happen here.

The air had become even chillier in the past few days, the season beginning to take full effect. I could feel the chill as I pulled my coat tighter around my body, hoping it did something to warm me up so that I didn't freeze before I made it to my dorm.

Oh you have got to be kidding me, I thought, as I stopped a few meters away from Zach, who was half hidden behind one of the main buildings. I was about to walk faster, to try and get away before he saw me when I heard him yell into the phone.

"You said you wouldn't get involved!" he growled. I had never heard Zach sound so angry before. He seemed frustrated enough that I didn't really mind that I was being rude, as I quickly made my way to the other side of the building, out of his line of vision. I didn't want him to see me and think that I had been eavesdropping. Actually, I didn't want him to see me at all, because I didn't want to talk to him.

The only downside to being trapped on this side of the building was that if I wanted to get back to my dorm quickly, I would have to walk straight past Zach, who I was sure would stop me before I had made it two steps. I didn't want to make the walk back to Quinn's dorm and I definitely didn't want to stay here and risk getting caught snooping on Zach's conversation. My only option was to pull up the hood of my coat and hope that by some miracle he didn't notice me.

His scream of frustration had my legs moving on their own accord as I power-walked past the building, holding my breath in hopes that if I didn't make a sound he would let me go. I didn't want to look, though it sounded as if he had thrown something at the wall, as the loud thud and cracking noise rang out. I just kept walking. I had walked a solid ten meters or so when I allowed myself to relax.

"Roux?"

Big mistake.

"Roux!" he called out. I acted as if I hadn't heard him and continued speed walking. However, I heard his fast footsteps catch up to me in no time.

"Roux," he said breathlessly as he grabbed my arm. I stopped and turned to him slowly. His face had been wiped clean of his anger, instead curiosity filled his eyes. "Sorry, if you overheard my conversation," he said sceptically.

I looked at him with faux confusion for a second before I tilted my head to the side.

"What?" I asked dumbly while trying my best to seem unaffected by his scrutinising gaze.

"Oh, never mind then," he mumbled as a grin overcame

his face. "Can I walk you back to your dorm?" he asked.

I knew I would sound like a terrible person if I said no but I really didn't want to deal with having to turn him away once we got there. I knew that there would only be one reason for him wanting to take me home and that was so that he could come inside with me.

Sighing, I nodded my head before I began walking again.

"Sure," I whispered quietly.

He chuckled as he walked alongside me, jumping about like a child.

"Where are we going?" he asked randomly as he stopped on the path. "Not taking me somewhere to kill me, are you?" he joked. I tried my best to squeeze out a laugh as I realised the situation I had gotten myself into.

"Actually, uh, my new dorm room is this way," I mumbled as I pointed to the building in the distance.

It was as if his face was immediately wiped of any happiness as he looked between me and the building.

"Is this because of the break in? Did something else happen?" he asked quickly.

I immediately shook my head, closing my eyes so that I could roll them without feeling bad.

"No, no, um after what happened, there were just so many reporters. It was only supposed to be temporary, but with what happened with my dorm, I don't know, it's just a good thing I was moved before then," I shrugged.

The concern on his face never left, however, he nodded slowly as he turned back down the path, his hands being shoved deep into his pockets.

"Oh, okay good," he mumbled and started walking faster to meet my strides.

"So how have you been doing?" he asked softly, kicking a rock off of the path.

How had I been doing? I wasn't sure. Today had been great, the past week however...not so much.

"Good," I answered, shrugging my shoulders.

"That's...good," he muttered awkwardly as we neared the building.

"Studying has been taking up most of my time," I lied as we walked through the carpark.

"Oh don't even get me started." He laughed. "This engineering course has me beat. You would think there would be one class in the whole degree that I'd enjoy, but no."

I wasn't sure what to say but was so thankful that the doors of the entrance were just up ahead.

"Maybe, I could come up?" he asked hopefully, scratching the back of his neck as a blush found its way to his cheeks. *Damn.* This was exactly what I hadn't wanted.

"Zach," I muttered softly as I looked up at him. He was tall, but nowhere near the size of Declan. "I don't know if that's such a good idea."

It was as if a switch had been flicked in his demeanour, arms crossed over his chest and a frown settling on his face.

"And why is that?" he asked cautiously.

I wasn't sure how I was meant to explain this to him without hurting his feelings, however I hoped that he took it the right way.

"Zach, I don't know if we should do this anymore..." I started, looking down at my feet, which shuffled nervously against the gravel road. "I um, I went on a date the other day with someone. It was actually really nice." I smiled. "I don't think it's going to be anything serious but, I still wouldn't feel right going on dates with a man while I'm in bed with another," I muttered.

"But what about this?" he asked, motioning between us.

I drew in a long breath and tried not to feel bad.

"Zach, we both agreed in the beginning that feelings

weren't to get involved," I said sternly. "That's why we both agreed to this, remember?"

His shoulders sunk as he let his head drop to the floor and my stomach tightened with guilt at his defeated look.

"Yeah I know," he mumbled. "Still doesn't make it suck any less though."

"Zach," I whispered, pushing his shoulder jokingly. "Come on."

"Come on? Seriously Roux? You can't just dump all of this on me and then play it off like a fucking joke," he scoffed. I flinched at his outburst, taking a step back as my eyes widened. What the heck just happened?

"What?" I asked, pulling my jacket tighter around me.

"I was the one who was always there for you, I'm the one who has been looking out for you and you go and choose some hot shot lawyer? What, is it his fancy car or something?" he asked, face growing grim.

"Zach. Don't," I warned.

"Don't what?" he asked. "It's not that hard to get you into bed, but what, it's hard for you to get into relationships. Then some rich lawyer comes around and suddenly you're all ready to settle down and take things slow?"

I hadn't met this Zach before. The Zach that said such mean things and I sure as hell didn't like him.

"Me not wanting to be in a relationship with you doesn't mean I can't be in one with someone else," I muttered lowly, backing away from him, trying not to show the hurt I was feeling.

"If only you knew Roux-"

"If only I knew what, Zach?"

He shook his head, a sneer staring back at me.

"That me and him aren't so fucking different."

I scoffed, stepping away from him and turning to walk

towards my building. How on earth had that managed to blow up so badly? *Me and him aren't so different, please, as if!*

"Roux," he called, his voice sounding just as hurt as I felt. I didn't bother to stop and listen.

CHAPTER 20

I spotted Quinn's head over the mass of students in the hall and pushed my way forward. I had been itching to catch her after last night's fiasco with Zach and I knew she wouldn't believe it. Tea was her specialty and the type I was serving was exactly her flavour.

"Quinn." Man this girl had to be deaf. "Quinn!"

Her pretty ponytail spun dramatically as she turned and eyed the crowd of people trying to spot me. Throwing my hands up in the air to catch her attention, I shuffled in between the other students.

"Hey," I whispered breathlessly when I made it to her side.

"Morning," she greeted with a smile. "Wanna grab a coffee? I'm meeting Will at Casper's."

I hadn't been to Caspers since the incident and just the mention of it had my stomach growling in submission.

"Yeah," I laughed. "Oh wait," I gasped, wiggling my eyebrows at her. "Is this a date?"

She laughed as her eyes rolled in her head.

"If this was a date, my beautiful, stupid Rouxette, you would not be coming along."

I gave her my most offended look as I placed my hand over my chest, my mouth slung open and eyes wide.

"Ouch."

She just laughed and dragged me along.

"As if you wouldn't do the same thing," she said.

She was right, but still.

She took my arm in hers and helped me weave through the others, breaking free of the crowd as we exited the main building.

"So I have some hot goss," she smirked as she pulled me down the path that led to Casper's.

"I think mine will be better," I mumbled, trying to keep up with Quinn's pace.

"I don't know," she mused, raising her eyebrows. "I got my final performance audition dates," she sang happily.

Gasping, I threw my arms around her.

"Oh my gosh! That's great, Quinn!" I laughed. She had been excited for her final performance since first year, I was happy that she could finally try out for it.

"Mhmm." She smirked. "Now I just have to get the lead."

I couldn't help but roll my eyes at her, she was a shoo in for the position by a mile. Everyone knew how great Quinn was, especially when it came to performing. Being dramatic was in her nature already.

"What yours?"

"Hmm?" I asked, kicking a pebble from the path.

"Your gossip?" she asked again, raising her eyebrows as if I was being an idiot.

"Oh." I laughed. "Well, it's definitely not as fun as yours."

"Oh come on!" She groaned, letting her shoulders sag down to the floor as she pouted. "You never have any goss, humour me this once."

Yes, she was definitely going to get the role. Sighing, I shrugged my shoulders and shoved my hands in my pockets.

"I told Zach I wanted to stop seeing him last night," I mumbled.

"Finally!" she yelled, her hands fist pumping the air. "This wouldn't have anything to do with a certain lawyer now would it?" she asked, wiggling her eyebrows at me suggestively.

I rolled my eyes but laughed at her antics.

"Zach and I were going to end at some point anyway, but yes," I said, trying not to blush. "I'm not going to date Declan with another guy in the picture."

Her little squeal and tip toe dance had me shaking my head as we neared the café.

"So you guys are dating?" she squeaked, looking like her head was about to pop off her shoulders.

"No," I said quickly, shaking my head. "We've only been on the one date."

"Oh totally," she responded sarcastically, still spotting a cheesy grin on her face. "So how did he take it? Zack, I mean."

About as well as being hit by a truck, I thought.

"He basically said that it was funny how I only wanted to be in a relationship with a guy who has money." I shrugged. "So not that great I guess."

"What a butthole," she muttered, looking equally as annoyed as me.

"Yeah, told me I was easy to get into bed too." I laughed rolling my eyes. "I guess he's not completely wrong," I joked, trying to lighten the mood. "But still a stupid thing to say." I smiled, eyeing Casper's just up ahead. I could see Wills mop of hair inside the window at the usual booth.

"Well, I'm glad that you cut that butt-crack loose," she said confidently, rolling her eyes.

I didn't answer, shaking my head at her whilst smiling. She was a complete psycho, but man she made things funny.

The bell to Casper's dinged familiarly as we walked in, the café being surprisingly empty compared to usual. Other than Will, who looked up at us, or rather Quinn, with a big smile, there were only one or two other students, too wrapped up in their conversations to even blink our way as we entered.

"What's up?" Will drawled stupidly as we sat down. "I'm thinking we have a coffee, we head back to yours, we get a little bit funky and we remember nothing in the morning, y'all in?" he joked as he threw up a finger gun at us.

"You're an idiot." I chuckled as Quinn cracked up beside me. "It's the beginning of the week."

"Yeah," he defended in a 'duh' tone, "perfect time to start the week off with a bang," he sassed, eyebrows raised. I just rolled my eyes, ignoring his childish behaviour.

"You have a test to study for," Quinn said in a serious tone, staring at Will for a second too long before a grin busted onto her face.

"You guys are lame," Will joked, pulling a face at Quinn. It was odd seeing two so casual around each other. Usually they were sounded by so much sexual tension you could hardly talk, however, it seems that since their confession, everything had settled down. *Thank the Lord*. I wasn't sure if I could take another movie night of side glances and 'accidental' touching. The whole campus needed this. I needed this.

"So did you hear about butt-crack?" Quinn asked loudly and I shoved her, looking around to make sure no one was looking at us funny. She just rolled her eyes, acting as if she hadn't just yelled the word butt-crack in a café.

"Is this that guy you're seeing?" Will asked, looking at me.

I rolled my eyes at him too, shaking my head. "It was one date!" I defended myself.

"But no," Quinn cut in. "Im talking about Zach."

"Oooohhhh," Will mused, sitting further on the edge of

his seat, eyes wide. "Do tell."

Oh my gosh, I thought with a smile, *these two really did deserve each other.*

"He called Roux a gold digger because his scrawny ass couldn't have her," she said, throwing her hair over her shoulder sassily.

"Quinn," I grumbled, rolling my eyes. "It wasn't that bad," I muttered.

"Puh-lease," she sang, "he's lucky I need to look good for my audition otherwise I'd have thrown hands with the guy."

"Really Roux, if you want me to have a word with him-"

"Thanks, Will," I cut him off, shaking my head at my two friends. "But I'm not worried, I'm sure he was just caught up in the moment and it doesn't matter anyway. It's not like I'm going to try and talk to him again."

"Good," they both said at the same time, before looking at each other with smiles on their faces. Oh gosh, maybe I did prefer the tension.

I jumped out of my seat quickly as my phone started ringing, thankful for the opportunity to get away from the lovebirds. I was even happier as I saw the name scrolling across the screen.

Mum.

"I'll be back in a second," I called, rushing out of the café, wasting no time in hitting the answer button.

"Hey Mum." I smiled as I pressed the phone to my ear.

"Rouxette sweetie, how are you?"

Well I got shot the other day, I thought, however, kept my mouth shut. My mother would not be able to deal with hearing that.

"I'm good." I laughed, sitting down on the bench beside the path.

"That's good to hear, how's school going, how's Quinn?" she asked.

"School's going okay, a little boring but you know how it is, studying hard," I said, feeling semi guilty when I realised I in fact hadn't been studying as hard as I should have been. "Quinn's great, finally got the date for her final auditions."

Her gasp led into a small squeal.

"Oh I'm so excited!" she cheered. "You'll have to give me the dates of her performance!"

How my mother managed to get along better with Quinn than she did anyone her own age I will never understand. They had grown fond of each other from the moment they were introduced. Of course, my mother grew fond of most people she met. She was a people person in a way I wasn't sure I would ever be able to be.

"Sure Mum." I laughed.

"When are you coming to visit?" she asked in a hopeful voice that always managed to make me feel terrible, even though I knew that wasn't what she was trying to do.

"You know how busy uni gets, Mum." I laughed, watching as a bird landed on the path in front of me. "I promise I'll come down in my break."

"But that's so far away," she grumbled, yet I could hear the smile in her voice. "Maybe I could visit you?" she asked hopefully. *Hm. My mother, my unexplainable new dorm room, Declan and the possibility of her finding out about the incident.*

"Maybe," I squeezed out, trying to sound as calm as possible.

"Yay," she cheered on the other end. "I'm not sure when exactly I'll be able to head up," she rambled, "probably some point in the next few weeks and I'm not sure for how long but I'm so excited to come and see you I feel like I haven't seen you in ages!"

"Mum," I said as she took a breath.

"Sorry." She laughed over the other end. "I just miss you."

"I know," I smiled. "I miss you too."

Someone walking up ahead caught my attention as my mother spoke about my old neighbour. Zach's familiar tattooed arm had me cringing as I looked around for the closest escape. I quickly moved from the seat and back to the front doors of Casper's.

"I've got to go, Mum," I cut in. "But I love you and I can't wait for you to come up," I rushed.

"Oh, okay sweetie, well, I love you too and say hi to Quinn for me! Have a good day, sweetie!"

"You too," I said quickly, hanging up the phone as I rushed into the building, over to the booth and jumped in quickly.

"What's going on?" Quinn asked confused with a smile on her face.

"Nothing, just Mum calling."

She made a face that screamed yikes as she nodded her head in understanding.

"So she still doesn't know about the whole…you know," she mumbled, putting her fingers up into a gun position.

"Nope."

"Well, that's always fun," she said sarcastically as she slurped down her smoothie. It was then that I realised my coffee sitting in front of me.

"You guys are the best." I sighed as I took a gulp.

I looked down as my phone buzzed, expecting a message from my mother. Instead, Declan's name flashed across the screen and I opened his message, making sure that neither of my dramatic friends were looking.

'Tomorrow night, dinner?'

Such a boy. It was hardly a sentence, let alone a good enough question to ask me out to dinner with. However, I eyed my friends, responding quickly.

'That depends, is this a date?'

His response was quick, bringing a smile to my face.

'Definitely.'

CHAPTER 21

I was sure I had been in the shower for at least half an hour, scrubbing, shaving and moisturising. I wasn't sure why I was feeling so on edge for tonight. I had been on a date with Declan before, it had gone well and I hadn't felt nervous at all. It wasn't as if this was our first date. Yet as I washed the berry shampoo out of my hair, I couldn't help but tap my foot on the bottom of the shower.

The shower would usually be my perfect place to relax, however, the longer I stood, the more wound up I could feel myself becoming. I didn't bother enjoying the warm water as I rinsed off and turned it off, jumping out and grabbing a towel quickly, before I grew cold.

I didn't waste time with my makeup, it was surely nearly seven now and I knew I would feel terrible for keeping him waiting. Even though I had most of the day to get ready, I still somehow ended up running late. Of course, it didn't surprise me in the slightest.

Tripping out of the bathroom door and stumbling to my cupboard I almost had a heart attack at the time. 6:45. I had fifteen minutes to get ready! I didn't bother looking through my wardrobe, I already knew that would waste too much of my time. Instead, in a game of Russian roulette with myself, I reached in and grabbed the first dress I saw. A simple grey slip dress. It would have to do.

I threw it over my head in a rush, trying to find a decent pair of shoes, deciding that heels in the mud outside would not be a good idea. I grabbed my black flats and my coat, throwing it over my dress in hopes that it would keep me warm in the weather outside. I could only hope that Declan had chosen somewhere warm for dinner. He had yet to reveal further about the venue, instead settling on telling me that the meal would be delicious and it was a surprise.

By the time I was wrapping my hair up in a low bun, I heard his knocks on the front door. My heart seemed to jump in my chest as I realised this was it. Again I scolded myself for feeling so silly, it was only Declan.

I quickly grabbed my phone, making my way to the door and pulling my phone tighter as the thunder crackled outside. I hoped wherever he was taking me was also inside. His smile greeted me as I opened the door, soon falling as he dramatically dropped his mouth open, making me blush.

"You look beautiful." He smiled, taking in.

My blush grew as it trickled down my neck.

"Thank you."

He seemed to enjoy my embarrassment, his smile growing to show his dimples.

"I'm sorry, I haven't been home to get changed yet," he chuckled, looking down at his suit wear. If only he knew that I really didn't mind.

"Did you just finish work?"

He nodded, moving out of the way as I shut and locked my door.

"It actually wasn't too bad today." He laughed. "A lot less drama than normal."

I laughed with him, as we made our way down the stairs towards the doors. By the time we reached them, the light rain outside had turned into a heavy thunderstorm. The downpour made Declan's car seem impossibly far away in the parking lot, we were sure to get soaked to the bone. Declan didn't seem to mind though, swinging the doors open and reaching over to tug me along to the edge of the covered area.

"Here." He laughed lightly, popping a small umbrella that I hadn't seen hanging from his other hand.

"Well, you really are full of surprises."

His light laugh became fuller as he chuckled at my teasing, shaking his head and tutting at me sarcastically.

"You have no idea," he smirked, pulling me unexpectedly under the umbrella and holding me tight, giving me no option but to move forward into the heavy rain with him.

The small umbrella did little to stop the rain from blowing into my face and nothing to stop it from soaking my shoes, yet I still found myself laughing with Declan as we ran for his car. He held the umbrella the whole time I got into the car, only moving it once I was securely out of the rain, before he ran around to the drivers side and jumped in.

The seats were nice and warm on my cold legs, quickly defrosting the chill the night air had left behind.

"So, now are you going to tell me where we are going?" I asked hopefully, giving the most convincing grin I could muster while my teeth chattered.

"Mmmm, nope."

I tried not to groan as I rolled my eyes. He didn't seem to care though, chuckling as he fiddled with the radio, the music filling the car quickly, probably in hopes that I would stop asking questions.

The early night traffic was hustling around us as Declan drove through the city. It seemed that no one here ever stopped, always on the run to or from something. We didn't have to navigate through the crowded lanes for long though as Declan exited onto one of the smaller main roads that lead to the nearby suburbs.

"We're not going for dinner in the city?"

His long sigh led to him shaking his head as he gave me a jokingly exasperated look.

"We're having dinner at my house, if you really must know Miss Fallon," he scolded, rolling his eyes as a smile fell upon his lips.

Oh.

"You don't live in the city?"

He shrugged, fingers drumming against the leather steering wheel.

"My line of work requires me to have an apartment in the city in case something comes up, I usually will take business partners there instead of the lake house. But I try to stay out here as much as I can, it definitely is a lot more peaceful."

He was right about that, it was already starting to look less like the cityscape and more like a tighter, cluster of towns. You could even almost see the stars as we drove, silently listening to the music dance through the car. Each time Declan would make a turn, the road would grow smaller and the building would grow fewer. I tried not to feel jealous about the open area around us that he got to spend his time in, I had wanted to escape that when I left for university. Now however, the thought of going home to the familiar diners and bookstores had my toes curling.

We turned onto a small dirt road with a mailbox at the front and I tried not to laugh at the mundanity of it all, this was definitely not what I had been expecting from Declan.

The further we trailed up the winding driveway however, the more I started to realise how wrong I was. The trees that encapsulated each side of the driveway hid the view of the house from us until the last second, when the tall building jumped out from the shadows and stood bare in front of us. The house itself was huge. I guessed that Declan used the term 'lake house' loosely, because to see this seemed more like the kind of mansion you would find in the pages of a book and less like those of the surrounding neighbours. The lake rippled under the weight of the rain and my door opening reminded me to close my mouth at the sight.

Declan held a hand out for me, the umbrella in the other. Eyeing me and the house as if he was expecting me to critique it. It looked old, the stone exterior seeming to blend in with the darkness and storm. The balcony however couldn't be missed, seeming to stem off what looked like a solid glass dome on top of the house. I could definitely see myself sipping a glass of wine on a balcony like that someday, writing peacefully as the weather passed by me.

"You like it?" he asked, pulling me towards the large front door.

Even the pebbled path leading to the steps seemed to fit the exterior designs.

"Yes."

Whoever had done the landscaping had been extremely good in their field.

Declan swung the door open easily, walking in and pulling me along. My heart jumped as I walked into the house, taking in the beauty of it as I was tugged through the short hallway. The ceilings were huge and white, making the already large house feel spacious. I hadn't expected it to seem so modern inside, the small hallway leading to an open room with possibly the largest kitchen to one side that I had ever seen. *Who on earth needed so much room?*

"Are you okay?" Declan asked. I realised he had made his way to the kitchen in the time that I had been rudely staring into the abyss of his house.

"Yes, it's just…wow." I laughed.

"I know, it's a bit much." He laughed. "But my father built it, so you know." He shrugged.

"I'm jealous," I joked, looking around.

He laughed with me, chopping something on the kitchen bench, the knife hitting the chopping board being the only sound surrounding us as I sat on the stool at the bench, watching him work expertly away at the onions.

"I heard what happened to your old dorm," Declan said, looking up from the bench. "Mr Thox called to inform me that the arrangements he had been making to reassign it to you would have to be put on hold until further notice."

I eyed him suspiciously as he grinned.

"Did you-"

"No," he laughed. "I may be a little out there but I wouldn't do that just to get my way." He laughed. "But about the room Roux, you can stay there for as long as you want, really, you don't need to feel bad. Technically at the moment it is still under the scholarship payment my firm gave to the school anyway, so don't feel like it's an issue. When your dorm gets sorted and everything is fine, we can talk more about arrangements, okay?" he asked thoughtfully.

It was as if a weight had been lifted off of my chest. The thought of not having to stress about my living situation anymore had me grinning from ear to ear. It wouldn't be too long surely, and I could go back to living with Quinn.

Just like that, this date had topped the first.

"Thank you."

He just rolled his eyes and smirked, going back to the onions on the chopping board.

CHAPTER 22

The pasta he had cooked was delicious. The large kitchen obviously wasn't just for show. I wasn't sure if I had ever eaten anything this good at a restaurant, let alone cooked by a guy on a date in his house.

"So Miss Fallon," he smirked from across the table. "Tell me about yourself."

"Like what?"

"Anything, hobbies, interests, friends."

I was fairly sure he already knew about my hobbies and interests, I was a fairly simple person with those. It was basically just writing and reading, if I was blog honest. *Damn, maybe I did need some other hobbies. Was I a boring person?*

"Well, I have a ridiculously crazy best friend, her name is Quinn. She's dating, well, kind of dating-I don't really know how it's working to be honest," I stumbled. "Anyway, my other friend that she's with, his name is Will, he's Chairman Thox's son. He studies chemistry at the university."

"Ah yes, the one we met in the hallway, right?"

"Yes." I blushed. Freaking Will.

"What about you?" I tried to divert.

He shrugged, taking a sip of his wine.

"Work keeps me pretty busy most days, I don't really have time for hobbies or friends."

"Yet you have time for this?" I asked, raising an eyebrow as I set down my fork.

His familiar smirk pulled up as he leant forward on the table.

"Always."

"You're an idiot."

It slipped out of my mouth quicker than I could stop it and I was stuck staring at him as he slowly processed what I just said.

His booming laughter filled the room soon after I saw the wheel stunting in his head and she looked at me like I had delivered him his Christmas presents early.

"Well." He nodded enthusiastically. "You're not wrong there!"

I felt as though I could catch on fire at any moment from the embarrassment coursing through my veins. *Why on earth couldn't I just be cool, for once in my life.*

"You really are something, Roux," he muttered, shovelling another forkful of his pasta into this mouth. I simply blushed harder.

He composed himself quickly, rubbing his hands over his face before resting them back on the table.

"What about guys, huh?" he asked, still chuckling lightly to himself. "You didn't want to go on a date with me because I would be a distraction, does that mean that you haven't done much dating before? No boyfriends?"

I tried not to look as surprised as I felt by his question.

"Uh-well, no," I stuttered. "I have had boyfriends before, only one serious one, but that was before university. I've been on a few dates but none of them really lead to anything," I mumbled. "When I said dating would be a distraction, I mean at the present time, not all the time."

"So you haven't been in a serious relationship since high school?"

I shook my head.

"Haven't found the right person."

He gave me a knowing look as he sipped some more wine.

"What was his name?"

"Hm?" I was confused.

"Your boyfriend, in high school," he smiled.

I laughed, thinking about how odd that sounded. Really it didn't feel like that long ago. Hearing someone speak about my dating habits in high school though made it sound silly and childish.

"Mike."

He nodded, seeming to mull over the name.

"What about you?" I asked, hoping to sound casual. "Any girlfriends?"

Surprisingly, he shook his head and eyed the table.

"No, my work doesn't usually allow opportunities for dating."

I raised my eyebrows at him.

"You're an exception," he rolled his eyes, smiling. "You were already dragged into it." He seemed to dislike what he said, eyebrows furrowing as he eyed me wearily. "Because of the incident," he clarified.

"Which one?" I joked. His frown turned upwards.

"True."

"Well, I'm glad that you decided to make an exception," I said softly, taking my first sip of the wine glass next to me, hoping that the usual blush didn't come creeping up my cheeks to ruin my boldness.

"So am I. We should do this again soon. I'm having a lot of

fun getting to explore you," he said softly, popping another piece of pasta into his mouth.

There was no way he meant for that sentence to sound so sexual. Surely. Yet the cunning glint that had formed in his eyes made it seem as though he knew exactly what he was doing. I decided to ignore the comment, in fear of only embarrassing myself more and shoved another forkful of pasta into my mouth, dropping my gaze as I caught him watching.

"Do you like it?"

I nodded, chewing quickly so that I could reply.

"Its delicious. I'm sorry that I wasn't very helpful in cooking it."

He waved off my apology, rolling up his dress shirt to reveal his tattooed forearms. I had to look away, to remind myself not to stare. *Oh my goodness. Why did he have to be so good looking. It just had to come in and complicate things, didn't it?* Still, my eyes slowly and cautiously made their way back to look at the intricate patterns on his arms. As quickly as I had tried to sneak a glance, he seemed to notice my staring, smirking at me from across the table as he sat his cutlery down. I lifted my glass to my lips and took big gulps, looking anywhere but him.

"It does seem to be getting a bit warm in here," he muttered. "Maybe I should turn down the heaters. Are you getting hot?"

I shook my head quickly.

"No, no I'm fine."

Little did he know I was getting very hot and flushed, however, I wasn't too sure it had anything to do with the heaters and perhaps more to do with what was now my empty glass of wine and his good looks.

"Are you sure? You seem a little flushed, do you want to take off your coat?"

Before I could say a word, he was getting out of his seat. My heart rate picked up as he walked closer to me, I stood to meet him, trying not to act as flustered as I felt.

"Let me help," he mumbled, moving behind me to slip off my coat. I could feel his breath on the back off my neck and tried not to move a muscle as he pulled it off. His fingertips grazed my skin as he removed it, the hairs on my neck rolling with goosebumps in an effort to stand on my skin.

"Better?" he asked, seemingly unaffected.

"Yeah," I whispered, turning around to take it from him, however, it was already sitting over the other seat.

He stood, looking down at me, seeming to be wondering just like I was, what to do in that moment.

Before I could even think to pull away however, he started to slowly lean in, his eyes scanning from my own down to my lips and back, seeming to ask permission for what he was about to do. I didn't bother waiting for him to come to me, body popping up on my tiptoes to meet him halfway. His lips tasted of the wine, sweet and strong as he slowly moved them against my own.

I had shocked myself in the moment, recovering quickly however, to move my own against his. The kiss soon grew more passionate. His tongue running quickly over my lip as I opened my mouth to give him access. My mind grew tingly as one hand came to cup my cheek gently, the other pushing the small of my back closer into him. He doesn't waste time exploring my mouth, expertly moving in ways that a small moan escaped from the back of my throat as I grew breathless. His thumb ran across my cheek as he pecked my lips one last time, pulling away to read his forehead against mine, looking into my eyes intensely.

"Are you trying to torture me?" he asked breathlessly.

I had no idea how to answer, opting to shake my head slowly, his eyes falling back down to my lips.

"Roux," he mumbled, biting his lower lip as his eyes met mine.

"Yes?"

His lips were back on mine in an instant. His hands gripping my waist softly, before I was lifted off the floor and rested sitting on the table. His hands moved up to my hair then, running underneath my bun effortlessly and causing my eyes to roll back. *Oh my God. He was going to be the death of me.* His lips moved quickly with mine, taking in as much of me as possible. His hand slipped down to rest on my thigh, rubbing circles into my skin.

He pulled away quickly, my phone on the table had started buzzing, startling us both.

"Im sorry," he mumbled. What had to have been a blush appeared over his cheeks and I couldn't help but laugh softly at his words.

"Don't be."

He eyed me with a soft smile for a moment, eyes searching my face for something that I wasn't quite sure of, before his attention turned back to the table.

"I should probably get you home soon?"

I eyed our empty plates and glasses, nodding.

"Thank you for dinner," I mumbled, slipping off of the table, to stand in front of him.

His grin grew bigger as he shook his head down at me.

"Thank you for everything else." He smirked.

CHAPTER 23

I waved Declan goodbye as he drove out of the parking lot. It was well past eleven by the time I walked into the dorm building but I didn't care. I needed to get into bed, call Quinn and spill the goss. For the first time I took the stairs two at a time, running my way up with pure excitement-driven adrenaline.

Someone on the third floor seemed to be having an argument in their dorm room and I concluded that the walls were in fact not sound proof and I would have to remember that for future arguments with Quinn. By the time I reached my floor I was puffed and hunched over but I didn't care. Tonight had been the most gossip worthy thing to happen to me in years and really all I wanted to do was call Quinn and have a good ramble about the whole thing. Most importantly, about Declan.

My ajar door put me off slightly as I made my way to the end of the hallway. I was so sure I locked it, I always locked it. I eyed it suspiciously, standing still. Declan had come, I had grabbed my keys and phone and then…maybe I didn't lock it. Perhaps I had been so wrapped up in Declan that I had forgotten to shut it completely?

After all no one other than Quinn, Will, Declan and myself actually knew which dorm room was mine, so it definitely wasn't Zach or someone trying to squeeze their way back in.

Shrugging I decided that if in fact there was someone inside when I went in, I would deal with it then instead of standing out in the cold hallway staring at my door.

The entry room looked like its usual self, nothing out of place. As I made my way through to the kitchen and dining room I was already shaking my head at my stupidity. There was nothing missing and nothing put out of place. No one had been in here. I was just simply incapable of performing a simple act liking shutting a bloody door upon exit.

Good on you Roux, great job, I thought to myself.

I made my way quickly to my bedroom, stripping and flopping down on my bed lazily as I crawled my way up and under the covers. By the time I had gotten comfortable and dialled Quinn's number, I was already yawning every other second of the dial tone. When it rang out, a pang of hurt washed through me, she never missed my calls. Then I caught the time on the nightstand. 12:01AM. Okay, so I definitely couldn't hold this one against her, she was definitely asleep.

Rolling over, I realised just how much the night had worn me down, my eyes fluttering shut quickly and my body screaming at me to relax. Sleep overcame me quicker than it ever had before, pulling me under in seconds.

My eyes snapped open, a bang waking me from my otherwise peaceful sleep. I sighed, my eyes burning with tiredness as I laid my head back down on the pillow, hoping that it overcame me as quickly as it did the first time. Then it happened again, and again. The banging sounded more like knocking hard and fast on my front door. My heart rate picked up. The clock on the nightstand read 2:45AM. There was no way none I knew would be knocking on my door so abruptly this early in the morning. I jumped, the knocks growing harder as my stomach rolled with the thoughts of who on earth was on the other side of the door. I had seen too many horror movies to ever go and check. I wasn't going to let whoever was out there know that I was awake and inside.

It was probably just a drunk student, who had the wrong floor and thought that my dorm was theirs, I reasoned as I laid my head back down on my pillow. My body buzzing from being abruptly awoken and stomach churning from my muddled sleepy thoughts on the masked serial killer behind the door. *Yep*, I thought. *I definitely have to go back to sleep.*

The open window had chills running up and down my spine as I pulled the blankets closer, too tired to consider getting up and closing it. I knew I would regret the decision in the cold hours of the morning, but that wasn't my problem right at that moment. I would allow my future self to get angry when she had to deal with it.

Trying not to think too much about the noise, I let myself slowly relax back into the bed. My head throbbing with my lack of sleep as it hit the pillow. It didn't take long for my eyes to slowly close again, unable to stay open any longer and my mind slipped away.

When I eventually did open my eyes for the second time, the sun was streaming in through the window and it was as if the odd encounter last night had never happened. There was no banging, simply silence and the far-off sounds of traffic to greet me. I grinned, wriggling around on the bed as I remembered the previous night. Spending time with Declan was starting to become a normal thing for me, I realised. I didn't mind though, he was right, sometimes distractions were good. I wasn't sure when the last time was that I woke from a sleep feeling fully rested. Yet, this morning I felt awake, full of energy and ready to take on the day. It was happiness, I realised. I was feeling utterly happy for once.

I didn't waste time lying in bed, instead getting up and changing into some pants and a blouse, running out the door to go and find Quinn, who I was sure would still be excited to hear about what happened last night.

We had kissed! Properly! A proper steamy kiss that I was sure Quinn would squeal about. Heck, even I wanted to let a little squeak out over it!

I flew down the stairs of my building, running out into the campus and ignoring the odd looks I received from others. *I've got places to be*, I thought to myself, *there's no need to feel judged.* I already knew where Quinn would be, she would have gotten up early to go to the gym this morning and Casper's always followed her workout. Perhaps her sugar craving was why she was so hyperactive.

Her mop of hair was easily spotted as she exited the café, holding her cup of hot chocolate. In all honesty, she kind of looked a wreck. I guess that's what happens when you get up at six to go exercise though.

"Quinn!"

She spun on her heels quickly, visibly relaxing as she saw me. By the time I had reached her, her arms were thrown around me and she was hugging me tightly.

"Are you okay?" I asked, concerned.

"I don't want to talk about it," she grumbled, pulling back and taking a big swig of her drink. "Let's go hang at mine," she grumbled, pulling me down the path as she interlaced our arms.

"Are you sure you're okay?"

She looked like she was about to explode as she eyed me, seeming annoyed at my question.

"Yes," she muttered, dragging me quicker. She was obviously lying, however I didn't want to push it further. She didn't seem like she was in the mood for talking.

"I went on another date with Declan last night," I offered, hoping she would bite at the distraction.

She spun quickly, letting go of my arm and crossing hers over her chest as she huffed and glared.

"I tell you there's something wrong and that I don't want to talk about it and your immediate response is to start talking about yourself?" she bit out, her lips pursing as she rolled her eyes.

I knew this was because she was upset, so I let it slide.

"Honestly Roux, could you be any more freaking self-centred? Maybe I don't want to talk about your amazing love life with Mr Hotshot Lawyer, maybe I don't want to even think about relationships at all right now, did you ever think of that?" she yelled, seeming to grow more frustrated with every sentence. "Ugh." She groaned, her head falling into her hands.

"So something happened with Will?" I asked.

She ignored the question, looking at the floor as she thought about something that I knew nothing about.

"Oh come on..." I tried to lighten the mood. "It can't be that bad, you guys are Quinn and Will."

The glare that fell upon her face had never been directed at me before. It made me want to curl up in a ball and roll away.

"Quinn I-"

"Shut up, Roux!" she screamed, tears finally breaking free from her eyes. "This is all your fault! You're the one who made me send that stupid message to him in the first place, you're the one that kept pressuring me into telling him and now everything is ruined! Just leave me alone! This is none of your business!"

By the end of her tantrum, sobs wracked her body as she gave me one last dirty look and stormed away. I stood still, watching as she retreated, trying not to feel as hurt as my chest was making me. It's fine, I tried to reason. She's your best friend, she will be back.

I realised my breathing was coming out quickly and I tried to reel it in before the inevitable tears came. I put my head down as I quickly walked away from where I had been stuck staring after her. *She's just hurt*, I reminded myself, *she didn't mean it.* Of course it didn't matter if she meant it, she had said it, and that alone was enough to have the wheels turning in my head. She was right, I had pressured her into telling him but it was a good decision. Or had been, until whatever had happened between them. I couldn't help but feel guilty now though, it was my fault that they were even together for whatever happened to happen.

My feet moved quickly to my dorm room, trying to bypass anyone who looked my way quickly. I was sure that if anyone caught my gaze I wouldn't be able to hold back the flood of tears that was quickly pooling in my eyes.

As I escaped the other students on the path, I broke out into a run, heading quickly for the cover of my dorm room. Taking the stairs three at a time, I made my way to the top, the tears finally releasing and falling down my face in hot streams as I trudged forward. Shiny boots caught my attention though, and as I looked up to the face of the person standing outside my door, looking at me in bewilderment, the sobs that I had been holding back broke loose.

"Mum."

CHAPTER 24

The one thing I loved most about my mother was her kindness. It especially came in handy, as she brewed a coffee in my kitchen, having sat me on the sofa with a kiss on my forehead.

"Now I'm not going to ask what happened, because I know you don't want to talk about it, but is there anything I can do to help?" she asked, walking over with a mug in her hands.

I smiled at her gratefully and shook my head.

"It's okay," I mumbled, taking a sip. "How did you know I had moved?"

She just shook her head, rolling her eyes. We definitely had that in common.

"When you weren't in your old dorms, I thought maybe you were in a lecture so I went to see administration. I was a little shocked when they said that you had moved dorms, even more when I got here," she said, looking at me curiously.

I wasn't really sure what to say so I just shrugged, leaning into her in the lounge.

"It's a long story."

Her soft giggle had my body sagging against hers and I couldn't help but smile.

"It always is," she joked. "This place is nice though," she mused, looking around the room. "I could nearly move in."

I knew she was joking, though I also knew that she was extremely curious as to how my room had been upgraded so dramatically. I didn't want anything regarding Declan up in conversation however. Her lead to the incident and I wasn't getting into that right now. Not when I felt so emotional. From Declan to Quinn to even Zach, it seemed like my whole month had been spinning out of control and I needed to get a grip on it before I could speak to my mother about anything and throw myself somewhere I wouldn't be able to handle.

"Why did you come Mum?"

"Can I not come and visit my daughter who never comes to see me anymore?" She pouted sarcastically.

"Mum," I groaned, turning around to grin at her. "I came to visit you last break."

"That was the last break! That was like two months ago Roux."

"Sorry," I smiled, rolling my eyes.

"Well, since I made the treacherous drive here and you don't want to tell me why you are so upset, why don't you take me out and show me the city?" she asked.

My mouth fell open as I looked at my mother, the drive here was only forty five minutes at best but I knew she hated traffic. Although she had made the drive to my university a handful of times before, she had never asked me to take her into the city. My mother and crowded spaces didn't mix, especially when it came to the big buildings and concrete floors. The city may as well have been a jungle for her.

"What?" I asked suspiciously.

Her little smirk had my mind thinking of Declan, I hadn't heard from him since last night.

"What? I can't spend time with my daughter?"

"Okay," I dragged out. "But if you think you're getting any gossip out of me for this, you're very wrong." I laughed.

Her face reddened and I gasped, pointing at her accusingly.

"I knew it!" I laughed.

She smiled and waved me off.

"Go get ready, we're still going."

I rolled my eyes and grabbed my phone and keys, shaking my head at her antics. She was already waiting at the door, unusually eager to get out and about.

It was obvious when we arrived in the streets of the city that she hadn't been here enough, her constant apologies for bumping people had me blushing every time.

"So what do people do out here for fun?" she asked, eyeing the traffic as we entered the main section of the city centre. I was sure there was more traffic here than she had ever seen.

"I know there's no open fields or swimming holes, Mum but there's still fun things to do."

She just rolled her eyes and pulled me along. It was odd to think about our small-town life now that I lived in such a large city. The summer nights I spent out in the middle of nowhere around a bonfire were some of my happiest memories, and yet I still found myself enjoying the city life more than I ever thought possible. Although, I did miss the stress-free times of swimming at dirty water holes drinking cheap beer with my friends. I wasn't really close with any of them anymore, most had all met me through Mike, so when we had split up when he left for university, they had slowly dwindled away, going their own separate ways as time went on. I wasn't sad about it, I had Quinn and Will, well, usually. Though the memories did make me feel a sense of nostalgia, for the simpler small-town life I had once lived.

"Why don't we go in there, that looks fun," my mum cheered, pointing to one of the largest shopping centres in the city. I smiled, shaking my head at her.

"Sure, Mum."

I looked around as we walked up the large steps to the entrance of the building, only in that moment realising how close Declan and I had been all along. I had been to this shopping centre more times than I could count with Quinn and Will, yet across the street stood a building almost as tall as the one we were about to enter. At the top, in big bold letters stood 'MARCELO'. A smile instantly made its way to my face as I realised that he was probably in there, working away at the endless list of jobs he must have had to do. Even whilst I found it funny that we were so close, I couldn't help but gulp as I turned back to my mother and walked in the store. If she ever found out about us, or how we met both the first and second time, she would surely lose it.

No, I thought. They wouldn't be meeting any time soon.

"I really do need some new covers for the cushions in the sitting room," she mumbled, eyeing the various stores on the first floor in astonishment. To be fair the amount of shops within the centre was a little extra, of course when you were catering to people such as Quinn, one couldn't help but go a little over the top.

"Is it in sections?" she asked as she slowly walked between the other customers.

"No," I mumbled, pulling her over to the information station. "But you'll find where everything is here, just type in what you're looking for and it will show you where to go."

"Well, that's a little fancy!"

I blushed, looking around at the other people while she typed away. When I realised she was typing the word 'cushion covers' instead of the name of a store I snickered, laughing at her as I showed her what to do.

"Oh," she muttered, her cheeks tinged pink as she looked at the map showing the way to one of the stores.

"Come on," I chuckled, pulling her down the path that the machine had set out for us.

"You must do this a lot, right?" She giggled, looking up towards the upper levels.

Surprisingly, I hadn't been shopping in a while. Usually Quinn would have pulled me and Will along for days out and shopping sprees, lately though she had been a little too consumed with her courses to focus on her 'window shopping'. Which wasn't necessarily a bad thing, with her spending habits.

"Sort of," I mumbled, walking into the store that we tracked down. I could see her eyes light up with the variety of homeware within the store. If there was one thing I didn't miss about my small town, it was the fact that it had absolutely no decent stores.

It wasn't long before she was dragging me all over the place, making me help her track down stores that sold things from kitchen appliances and hair care products.

We passed a large bookstore, with a mass of people inside and my mother stopped us to point.

"Do you want to go in?" she asked, wiggling her eyebrows at me.

I couldn't help but think of the small bookstore which Declan had taken me to, the lack of people yet the abundance of invitation it held. Of course, that led to the stack of books that Declan had bought for me, that were currently sitting in a pile in my bedroom. I really didn't need any more any time soon.

"No that's all good." I shrugged, pulling her along to find the next store she would be entranced by.

"Are you sure, sweetie?"

I wasn't surprised by her confusion, I almost always jumped at the opportunity for new books.

"Yeah, I have a lot at home. Do you want to go in there?"

My mother eyed the boutique with wide eyes.

"Yes!"

It was roughly an hour later that my mother sighed, sitting all of her bags down on the floor beside the chair she sat on.

"I don't know how anyone could possibly visit them all," she marvelled, looking at the stores around us.

"They don't normally try." I laughed, picking up some of her bags.

It had grown slightly darker throughout the building, the automatic lights popping on to signal that it was starting to grow dark outside.

"We should probably get going soon," I said, showing her the time on my phone. 5:04. Definitely time to start heading home. I knew my mother didn't like driving home in the dark, which meant that she was probably going to spend the night at my dorm room, which wouldn't be an issue anymore, considering my large bed and how comfortable the lounge was.

The sun was only just peeking over the buildings as we exited. The early night air having grown even colder, I eyed my mother in her thin cardigan.

"Here."

I reached into the bag from the boutique, pulling out one of the thicker jackets that she had brought, handing it to her.

"Thank you." She smiled, her teeth already beginning to chatter.

I grinned, gripping the bags tighter as we went to walk

down the street, however, the breath seemed to be knocked out of me quickly, my feet planted firmly on the ground as I saw Declan exit the building across the street. I tried not to move, hoping he would keep walking and ignore us.

"Let's go," I mumbled softly. "It's getting cold."

As if hearing my voice, his head snapped our way, locking eyes with mine. His familiar smirk came over his face as I saw his eyes bounce from me to my mother. I tried to capture his attention silently with my eyes. Though, my subtle head shakes and warning looks didn't seem to faze him as I saw him start to cross the street.

I tried to pretend as if I hadn't seen him, my mother mumbling something as I pulled her quickly down the street. I hadn't made it far when a pair of brown leather shoes blocked my view of the ground. I didn't want to look up to see the face that I knew would be smiling down at me.

"Miss Fallon," he greeted. I could hear the smugness in his voice. I wanted to glare at him, however, as my mother poked my back, I couldn't help but glance up at him like a deer caught in the headlights.

Help me, I thought. *Please see that this isn't a good time!*

As my mother poked me in the back firmer this time, I let a forced smile come over my face.

"Mr Marcelo," I said politely.

Please let this go smoothly.

A smile instantly came over his features and I knew I was in trouble. His eyes quickly moved to my mother, who eyed us both curiously.

"You must be Mrs Fallon." He smiled, holding out his hand to my mother.

I didn't blame her for her mouth having slightly fallen open, he did look quite the sight in his blue suit and brown shoes, a brown leather satchel slung over his shoulder.

"Yes," she squeaked, smiling warmly at him.

"Mum this is Mr Marcelo," I said smoothly. "He is funding a scholarship for the English department this year."

Declan's eyes seemed to dance as he realised the white lie I was trying to get away with.

"Yes," he agreed confidently. "Of course Roux and I know each other a little better than that," he smirked, eyeing me as if seeing how I would react.

I wanted to strangle him as I burnt up in his gaze. My mother's growing smirk telling me that she had caught onto what he was throwing.

"She is one of the main candidates," he continued, smiling as if he hadn't almost given away our budding romance. My mother though, looked between us, eyeing me suspiciously as she smiled up at him. *Shit.* She knew there was something going on.

"Roux, why didn't you say anything." She smiled, motioning to Declan about the scholarship, however, I could tell by the glint in her eye that she meant something else entirely and found this situation much funnier than I did.

"You know," I struggled. "Study and stuff, must have slipped my mind."

I ignored Declan's gaze that was fixated on me as I eyed my mother, pleading with my eyes to get us out of here.

"Well, it was lovely to meet you Mr Marcelo-"

"Declan, ma'm," he cut in, smiling knowingly down at her.

"It was lovely to meet you, Declan," she corrected, grinning at him as if he was the best thing in the world. "But we must be getting home soon, I still have a long drive ahead of me."

My eyes widened at my mother's words. There was no way she thought I was going to let her drive back home at this time of day, especially with her lack of confidence in traffic.

"I better let you get going then," he apologised, stepping aside as he smiled down at us.

"It was lovely meeting you Mrs Fallon, I'll see you later, Roux," he smirked, as my mother tugged me along.

Oh so now you want to hurry, I thought, rolling my eyes at her, as she rushed us back to my dorm.

CHAPTER 25

I wasn't sure if my mother had ever asked me so many questions in my life. Between the walk home and dinner, she had managed to squeeze in a question regarding basically every aspect of any topic that I could possibly know. The first of which being, "So are you guys dating or is this casual?" Which not only had set my face on fire but had also been ten times worse because I had no idea how to answer it.

Declan and I had been on dates yes, so I wouldn't say we were just casually seeing each other, however, also hadn't established that we were 'dating' yet, which I was actually quite happy about, however, my mother on the other hand had taken this silence for a heck ton more than what it had been, screeching as she threw her hands up in the air.

"I knew it!" she screamed. "My baby's got a boyfriend!"

"No!" I had quickly cut in, hyping to stop this madness before it had even begun. "We have been on some dates yes, but we are not together."

Her smile flopped as she looked at me, her face morphing

into a 'you better get a bigger shovel if you want to have that much crap' look, making us both roll our eyes.

"That makes no sense," she muttered in confusion.

"Yes it does!"

"No, either you guys are going on dates and dating, or you guys are just hanging out as friends," she said confidently.

"There is so much wrong with that sentence," I laughed.

"You kids confuse me," she mumbled, rolling her eyes as she grabbed the rest of her things.

"Are you sure you can't stay the night?" I asked, honestly scared that she wouldn't be able to handle the nighttime traffic heading out of the city.

"Roux, sweetie, you know I would love to but honestly I need to get back to the gallery tomorrow morning."

I sighed, hugging her as she made her way to the door.

"Please be safe."

She rolled her eyes, pulling me in for another hug.

"I'm a grown woman." She laughed. "I'm sure I can make it out of the city in one piece."

As the door opened she sighed, giving me her most motherly look.

"Everything will be fine with Quinn sweetie, it'll sort itself out." She smiled.

My eyebrows creased.

"How did you know?"

She smiled, shaking her head.

"I'm your mother, Roux, but other than that it clearly isn't boy issues and I doubt it's school, that leaves Quinn. Which you don't need to stress about, she's your best friend, you both will get over it soon enough."

"Thank you," I whispered, pulling her back in for one last hug before I pulled back and blinked a few times, making sure I didn't cry again. I hadn't realised how much I had missed her in the short time that we had been apart. It was funny how she always seemed to bring a sense of comfort into my life, making me feel as if everything would be okay.

"Bye sweetie." She smiled, kissing me on the cheek before spinning and walking out the door, giving me a small wave.

However, when she was gone, the comfort I had been feeling began to quickly drain away, leaving me looking around at the empty dorm room in distaste. I missed Quinn, I knew she was probably missing me but I also knew that she would have called me by now if she was over it. Her lack of communication led me to believe that she must have still been caught up in her feelings. I just hoped she got over it soon so that we could make up and move on.

I had pulled my book bag out in hopes of getting some study done, when in fact I had found the book that I had been reading sitting longingly inside. I knew I needed to catch up on my studies, I knew that I should open up my textbooks and revise something, anything and yet I allowed myself to open the book instead, enjoying the simplicity of reading without feeling guilty.

It was about halfway through that my phone had started ringing on the bedside table beside me. When I saw that it was Declan who was calling, my face flushed, remembering how he had acted in front of my mother this afternoon.

I answered quickly, ready to give him a piece of my mind.

"Declan," I deadpanned.

"I'm happy to hear that you're not angry at me anymore."

"What the heck!"

"Okay, okay, I know and I'm sorry." He laughed. "You didn't exactly tell me that your mother was coming or that you would ambush me out the front of my work either though."

My mouth dropped open at the audacity he held.

"I did not-"

"Oh don't try to deny it, Miss Fallon," he joked. "We both know you enjoy my company enough to resort to stalking."

"Declan!"

His booming laughter filled my ears as I scoffed at him through the phone.

"You're crazy," I groaned, flopping back on my bed.

"Only for you," he said in a funny voice.

I rolled my eyes, an exasperated sigh falling from my lips.

"Okay, okay, I really am sorry."

"Sure you are." I smirked, my stomach growling as I made my way to the kitchen.

Dinner could be something easy tonight.

"Your mum seemed nice."

A packet of two-minute noodles greeted me from the cupboard and I snatched them quickly. Jackpot.

"She's probably the best person I know," I said honestly, agreeing with him.

The loud bang on my door had the noodle packet falling from my hands as I jumped.

"What was that?" Declan asked, his voice having turned stern and hard.

"Probably just someone trying to be an idiot," I gritted out, picking up my noodles from the floor.

"Go check," he said sternly.

"What?"

"Go and look through the peephole and tell me what you see."

I rolled my eyes, opening the noodle packet.

"Declan, it's nothing, there was someone doing the same thing the other night, I'd say one of the other students just likes being a-"

"Go check."

His tone left no room for arguments, so I huffed, feeling

slightly hurt by his abruptness. As I walked to the door and looked out the peephole I couldn't help but feel a little good about being right.

"Just like I thought," I smirked. Something underneath my foot crunched as I stepped back. The bright yellow envelope stared menacingly up at me as I looked down at it. It must have slipped under my door.

"Well, it's always better to be safe than sorry."

I ignored him as I picked it up, my name having been scrawled out messily. Surprisingly it hadn't been closed, the contents spilling out as I lifted it, scattering what seemed to be photos all over my floor. As I scooped them up and looked closer however, my breath caught as my heart race increased.

"Roux?"

I grew instantly dizzy, gripping the bench top for support as I looked down in my hands. That was me. Those photos were all of me. Seemingly unimportant snippets throughout what would have to be the past few weeks. Me and Quinn at Caspers, in my lectures, Declan and I on our date. What the fuck.

"Roux, what's going on?"

The further I looked into the pile the more my stomach grew violently unsettled. Pictures from the coffee shop, pictures with my mum.Someone had been…stalking me? The closeness of the pictures was what unsettled me the most. They all had to have been taken by someone who had been physically close to me. Someone on campus. I wanted to throw up, stomach tightening and head growing dizzy quickly.

"Declan," I whispered, my eyes landing on the sticky note stuck to the last photo.

"I'm here, what's wrong?"

Leave now and tell no one.

I was sure I was going to cry, my eyes stinging as I tried to make my frazzled brain spit out a sentence.

"I need your help."

"Roux, you need to explain to me what's happening, I'm on my way."

I grabbed my phone and the envelope, shoving everything back in as I fumbled with the door, wasting no time in leaving my dorm room.

"I think someone's been following me," I muttered softly, trying to make my way down the stairs quickly. "There are photos of me Declan, so many photos."

"Stay on the phone Roux," he sounded almost angry. "Where were the photos, where did you find them?"

"They were in my dorm," I whispered, my voice breaking. "Someone slid them under my door."

"I'm coming Roux."

I felt myself struggling to breathe but there was nothing I could do as I threw myself out of my dorm building. The cold night air gripped me tightly as I went to move forward, coming to the realisation that it was dark, cold and I had absolutely nowhere to go. Surely, nothing would happen in such an open space. Then, my mind reeled back to the incident and the fact that all the photos had been taken in completely public places.

I frantically looked around, no one else was in sight, yet I felt as though I was being watched. Hair standing up straight on my arms as goosebumps rippled from my scalp down to my calves.

"Roux?"

I tried to focus on his voice, he would be here soon, he would know what to do.

"I'm near the carpark."

"I'm almost there," he assured, and I felt a slight drop of relaxation ripple through me.

I jumped, someone walking around the corner of the building. My breath hitched, feet trying to run while my body made itself stay still. The couple eyed me oddly, hurrying off down the opposite path.

I let out a long breath, trying not to get too overwhelmed, headlights coming towards the car park drawing me out of my oncoming panic attack.

"Is that you?" I asked, hoping he said yes.

"It's me."

I didn't waste any more time, running towards his oncoming car as quickly as I could, meeting him in the middle as he threw my door open and I jumped in. Buckling quickly, whilst he sped away. It was then that I let myself go, tears streaming quickly down my face as the unleaded sobs wracked my body.

Declan eyed me quickly, his eyes wide and eyebrows furrowed.

"Did you see anyone? Was there anything else-"

"There was a note."

"What note?"

I scrambled to pull the small sticky note out of the envelope, Declan's eyes frantically moving from the road and back to me.

"It just says, leave now and tell no one," I scrambled, still stumbling to pull it out. "But there are these photos of me. Me with Quinn, me with my mum, with you."

"With me where?" he asked, I had never seen him so serious before. "At the lake-house, at the bookshop?"

"The café."

"That's all the note says?"

I double checked, turning it over.

"Yes." Then it hit me. "Oh gosh, you don't think they know I told you do you?"

"Whoever is doing this is doing it to scare you, Roux,

telling me was possibly the best course of action you could have taken."

"Scare me? Why?"

He huffed, looking conflicted as he eyed me cautiously.

"That's what we need to find out."

CHAPTER 26

I sat in Declan's lake house silently, knees wobbling. He hadn't left my side the whole time I had gone through what had happened with him, only leaving a few minutes ago to call someone who he insisted could help. I had no idea who it was, or how any of this for together, and I didn't understand why I would be a target in any of this.

I wasn't stupid, I knew I was boring person, someone that people hardly glanced at on campus, let alone went out of their way to stalk. None of it added up and I wasn't sure if I even wanted to know who was behind it.

"My brother is on his way, he can help."

His voice startled me from the doorway, causing me to jump.

"Your brother?"

I didn't know he had a brother, then again I didn't know much about his family, except for his father, yet here we were. I wasn't sure if I should have felt like an idiot for freaking out so much earlier, they were only photos after all. Although I knew I shouldn't have been too nervous, Declan was a lawyer, he had to have seen this type of thing before.

MARCELO

"He's a cop," Declan muttered, walking over to the small stand next to the lounge, pulling a glass from somewhere and filling it with what I assumed was whiskey. "You don't need to worry," he said softly, eyeing me with sincerity. "I won't let anything happen to you."

I was sure he couldn't promise that, although his words still resonated a feeling of comfort within me.

"You can't guarantee that," I mumbled, fiddling with my hands in my lap.

"I can guarantee that I will do everything in my power to make sure that nothing like this happens again. But you need to tell me if it does, Roux."

I simply nodded. Even with his added support, I couldn't help but think, what else did this person know? If they had been following me, they could have seen or heard anything. I mean I spoke to Quinn about everything and they had clearly been close to the both of us. They obviously knew where I lived, they knew who my friends were, my classes…*take a breathe Roux*, I thought to myself, trying not to get too worked up. Everything was going to be okay. Declan knew what he was doing.

"I'm sorry, for all of this," I mumbled, throwing my rosy cheeks down into my hands. This was not his problem to deal with.

"You did the right thing telling me, Roux," he said seriously, before leaning over slowly and placing a lingering kiss on my forehead. The contact had my body sagging, seeming to rid me of the adrenaline I had been running off.

I didn't get a chance to answer though, the lock at the door startling us both. Declan recovered quirky though, walking over and swinging it open to reveal a smaller man, however still well-built. His cropped hair looked nothing like Declan's, however his eyes matched perfectly.

"Dec..." He nodded, as Declan stepped away from the door, allowing him to enter.

As his eyes met mine though, his face struck recognition and I found my brain trying to search through my memories to where I had seen him before.

"We have a situation Derek," Declan grumbled, shutting the door quickly and coming to stand by my side.

I was much too caught up in this man's features to acknowledge Declan though, that face, where had I...oh my gosh.

"It's been awhile, Miss Fallon." He nodded politely.

I gaped at him. The police officer who had taken my statement the morning Declan had been shot. Declan had mentioned getting my name from my statement, from his brother. It was all starting to make sense.

"Why don't we go through what happened?" he offered.

When I didn't immediately reply, Declan took over, relaying what I had told him in the car. I listened and nodded when appropriate but hardly retained anything he had said.

"Is this all correct, Miss Fallon?" he asked, eying me carefully before looking at Declan.

"Yeah." I sighed, looking towards the floor.

"Has anything else happened that you may deem as out of the usual lately?"

My mind immediately went to the other night.

"I thought I had forgotten to lock my dorm door not too long ago," I cleared my throat. "When I got home the other day it was open, then there was some banging on my door late that night, it was loud and a bit odd."

"You didn't go to see who it was?" he asked suspiciously, his eyes narrowing at me.

I gripped the leather lounge under his intense gaze, the haze on my mind starting to clear with his scrutiny.

"It was late and I had assumed it was another drunk

student. Other than the fact that I was scared, I wasn't getting out of bed to go and see what was going on."

He nodded, jotting down something on his notepad.

"Do you mind if I take the photos with me? For evidence?" he asked, looking at Declan expectantly.

"Evidence?"

Declan turned, his small smile obviously trying to comfort me.

"This could be serious," Declan mumbled. "You should see what he can do."

I looked between the two, their eyes both intensely pressuring me to say yes. I didn't want this to be a big deal though, for all we know this could just be someone playing a terrible joke.

"Come on, Roux," Declan cooed.

"Okay."

"Do you have anyone you can stay with for the time being? A family member, a friend close by-"

"You can stay here," Declan cut in.

My eyes bulged at him in confusion.

"No, really, I'll just talk to administration-"

"You're not going back to your dorm, Roux, not until we have sorted this out and we know that it's safe. You can stay here, it has plenty of spare bed rooms." He left no room for argument but a huge space for my guilt. "I'll have someone pick up your clothes and necessities from your dorm, don't stress. I'll speak with the chairman, I'm sure he won't mind if you switch to online classes for the time being."

My mind spun with his words, trying to realistically think about everything he had just said. Online classes, moving in here, it was all so dramatic.

"I don't really think that's necessary," I mumbled, fumbling with my fingers.

"I suggest you take my brother's offer into consideration,"

the officer said. "I'm sure you feel very confused and on edge right now, but this is possibly the safest place for you, at least for the time being."

I nodded once, not wanting to seem ungrateful. Despair seeming to quickly pool in the bottom of my stomach. I didn't want Declan to feel that he was now on watch duty.

"Thanks…" I fumbled for my words. I knew his name had been said before, yet it completely slipped my mind.

"Derek." He laughed.

"Thanks. Derek." I smiled forcefully, all I wanted to do in that moment was curl up in a ball and cry and fall asleep.

"Don't feel bad," Declan said, surprising me, seeming to be able to read my expression. "I would rather know that you are safe here than take any risk in you going back to your dorm."

I nodded softly, allowing my gaze to flop back down to the floor.

"I better get going," Derek chimes. "I'll run some prints, see what we can find."

"Thanks," Declan said, patting his shoulder as he walked him to the door.

"It was lovely seeing you again, Miss Fallon," Derek called from the door. I smiled politely at him.

"You too."

As I heard the door shut, I let myself spin sideways, laying down on the lounge in defeat.

"As soon as this is sorted, I promise I will be out of here," I mumbled, closing my eyes as I felt him come closer.

"Roux," he muttered softly, crouching down beside me.

I could feel his breath on my cheek.

"There is no need to be stressing over staying here with everything else that is going on. I feel better knowing that you're safe, under my roof, with me."

I understood his determination to help me, this was his

job. It didn't make me feel any less terrible about the whole thing though.

"Let's get you to bed," he whispered, holding out a hand to help me from the lounge.

As we walked up the stairs and into a bedroom, I didn't have much time to think about anything, my head hitting the pillow, Declan's soft goodnight and then…sleep.

CHAPTER 27

*D*eclan was speaking with someone as I made my way down the stairs, my hair dripping cold water droplets down my back, a fluffy bathrobe wrapped securely over my undergarments. I had yet to receive any of my clothes and refused to put the ones on from yesterday, which must have reeked from the stressed sweat that they had been drenched in.

I could see Declan, blocking the doorway from my view, however, my bags sat at his feet and I released a sigh of relief at having my own clothes. His head whipped around, meeting my gaze and allowing me to see the familiar face. The man who had carried me to the hospital the morning I had been shot.

"But yeah, they trashed it," he mumbled, yet to see me standing behind Declan, who spun back around to nod and held his hand out for the man to shake.

"Thank you West, I'll be in touch."

The guy, West, merely nodded, his gaze meeting mine as he smiled politely, only to have the shut quickly in his face.

"He's one of my employees," Declan said, answering my

unasked question, as he picked my bags up from the floor and made his way over to me on the stairs. I nodded, my eyebrows crinkling in confusion. He had sent an employee to gather my things? I wasn't sure if it was odd or not, I mean who else would he have sent? Then again, perhaps a police officer may have been more fitting.

"Why would you ask an employee to get my things?" I asked, curiosity getting the best of me. Decals laughed, seeming to brush off my question with a raise of his eyebrow.

"Because he's my employee," he answered sarcastically.

I held back from pulling a face at him. *Yes,* I thought, *your employee at the firm, not for personal affairs.* However, I kept these comments to myself, my head already becoming pained with the oncoming headache, I didn't need to add any more pressure to it.

I rolled my eyes but followed him into the spare bedroom that he had showed me last night. He sat my bags down on the bed, smirking as he pointed to the door.

"I'll meet you in the kitchen."

I didn't bother answering as he swiftly made his way out of the door. Instead I focused my attention on my bags and unzipped them to find a good portion of my winter wardrobe packed away. There was no contemplating whether or not to put on my sweats, that I happily pulled out of the bag and stepped into. Throwing an old long-sleeved T-shirt over my head. The mirror beside the bed showed me just how much weight I had surprisingly lost over the past few weeks, the stress of study, Declan and Quinn must have gotten to me more than I thought.

I tried not to think about that though, as I made my way down to find Declan, hoping that he was cooking something as my stomach rumbled. He was pulling different things from the fridge as I walked in, turning slightly to smile at my outfit, before his head was back in the fridge.

"What would you like?" he asked.

"Whatever you're having is fine."

"Omelette?"

He sat the eggs and pan down on the counter with the other ingredients, looking at me for approval.

"Yeah."

As he began to get set up he eyed me standing awkwardly from the other side of the bench.

"Why don't you go and have a look around the house while I cook breakfast?"

I smiled, nodding before moving out of the room.

"I'll come get you when it's ready," he called.

I had seen many doors that lead to places I had yet to discover. My curiosity got the better of me, as I tried the first one I reached. The small door beside the staircase however, didn't budge as I tried the handle and I found myself frowning as I rolled my eyes, moving my way up the stairs instead.

The first few doors seemed to only lead to other bedrooms or bathrooms, all until I made it to the last door on the second floor, which held a small staircase inside. My interest peaked as I looked side to side before creeping in, shutting the door behind me. I felt almost like I was in a mystery movie and for a moment my worries faded away as I walked up. As my head popped into the small third story room, I felt as if I had stepped into a dream.

It was a circular room, all walls curved with floor to ceiling bookshelves. Bookshelves that were filled with more books than I had ever seen in a house. A small desk sat overlooking the balcony outside that faced the lake, and the sofas and coffee tables in the middle of the room looked to be the perfect place to sit and read. *Holy cow*, I thought. *I had never been more jealous of a house in my whole life.*

The best part by far though, the roof. Completely made of glass, showing a perfect view of the sky as the rain patted softly against it. *This is it*, I thought. *This is my perfect place. I want this. One day, when I'm rich and famous perhaps.*

"I was wondering when you would find this place."

I spun, to look at Declan who watched me as my eyes widened.

"Oh my gosh!" I whispered, turning to continue marvelling at the room.

"Your breakfast," he said, putting it on the coffee table.

I felt terrible for not reacting more politely towards the food but I couldn't pull my eyes from the shelves.

"My father spent a lot of time up here."

"I can see why." I laughed, making my way over to the lounges. "I think I'm in love."

He shook his head, smirking as he pushed my plate towards me.

"It's going to go cold."

"Sorry," I mumbled sheepishly. Pulling the plate forward, and taking a quick bite. It was delicious.

Declan sat quietly opposite me, eating his omelette as we listened to the sound of the rain.

"Tell me something," I said quietly.

His brow arched as he looked at me oddly.

"Like what?"

"Anything. Before last night I didn't know you had a brother. I hardly know anything about you and were going to keep…" I paused, my eyes going wide as I rethought my word choices. "Seeing each other. I think we should probably get to know each other a little more."

His familiar smirk overcame his face.

"Seeing each other?" he snickered. "You can say we're dating, Roux."

My face broke out in fire as I looked anywhere but him.

"Are we?" I asked meekly, my eyes quickly darting to his and then away.

He looked at me as if I had gone crazy.

"We're going on dates, aren't we?"

"Well yes…but you haven't, well you know…you haven't exactly made it official," I stumbled. "Not that I'm complaining!" I rushed. "I like taking things slow!"

He was in a fit of laughter before I had even finished speaking. Head thrown back, belly-laughing at me.

"What?" I asked.

"I just didn't realise I needed to make things official in order for them to be official. I like you Roux, I have since our first coffee date and I was sure I would when I met you in that hospital room. We can take things as slow as you like. But if I had known that I had to ask you to date me, I would have." He chuckled.

I wasn't sure exactly how to reply to him, my mouth hanging open as he eyed me with humour.

"I like you too," I mumbled, blushing as I quickly shovelled the last of my omelette into my mouth.

Declan's eyes caught mine in his intense hold as he watched me. I had never been watched in such a way. It was as if he was in awe of what I had said. It was obvious though, of course I had grown to like him over the time we had spent together.

"Well, in response to your question," he quickly recovered. "I'm not quite sure where to start. I have one brother, Derek, my mother lives in her home town in Italy, my father moved them back there a few years ago after he sold his last company so that they could be closer to her family."

I felt terrible. I had assumed his father was dead.

"He gave me this house as a parting gift." He chuckled, shaking his head. "He said I should find someone to appreciate it."

My cheeks grew hot at what he was insinuating and I moved my gaze to look out upon the lake. I definitely appreciated it.

The rest of the day had been spent lazing about in the reading room, waiting on a call from Derek. To be honest, after seeing this room and getting to spend the whole day doing nothing but reading with Declan, I hoped that he never called at all.

Declan and I sat at the dinner table, my eyes trained on the familiar pasta dish that sat in front of me. I wasn't sure if he had purposefully chosen this dish or if it was the only one he could make. However, the memories of his lips on mine after the last time we sat here like this, eating this exact pasta had me unable to look him in the eyes. He had to know. My face burned at the thought of him purposefully baiting me like this.

He eyed me knowingly from across the table, popping a piece of pasta into his mouth with a smirk. My cheeks were aching from holding back the smile that was trying to rip free on my face. I had to focus on my food. The food that Declan made. That he also made the last time that we were here. When we fade out on the table. *Shit.* Everything led to him.

"Miss Fallon," he spoke, staring me down with an evil glint in his eyes. "How's the pasta?"

I swallowed my mouthful, his eyes never leaving my face as I tried to think of something to say. Anything.

"It's delicious."

He slowly stood from his chair, reaching to the middle of the table where the bottle of wine sat unopened. *Oh no,* I thought, *not the wine.* He filled his cup before pouring a small amount in mine, eying me sheepishly.

"We wouldn't want you to have too much this time, now would we?"

I tried to cover my shocked choking noises with a cough, having no choice but to lift the glass and take a sip.

"You have hardly touched your plate, is there something wrong?"

He knew what he was doing. I was sure of it. His game of cat and mouse winding me up perfectly to his advantage. I tried to relax, taking in a big breath whilst I brought my own smirk to my face.

"No, I can't think of anything else, I'd prefer to be eating."

He hid his surprise well, the rosy colour of his cheeks, the only indication that he had picked up on what I meant. *Two can play at this game,* I thought with a smirk.

"Well, that makes one of us," he smiled and I found myself lowering my eyes to the table, my stomach starting to dip at his words. He was much better at this game than I was.

"I don't know why, it's delicious."

He eyed me, the wheels trying in his head as he clearly debated whether or not to press this further.

"I hope you understand just how much you affect me, Roux." He sighed, downing his glass of wine in one mouthful.

"I think I get it," I whispered, looking down at the floor.

If I was being honest he affected me in a way I hadn't ever felt before. His mere teasing comments were enough to get me so wound up that I was sure in a minute I would have to excuse myself before I burnt up from my blush. Before I knew it he was in front of me, holding a hand out to help me from my seat. I took it, unsure of what was happening, when he pulled me up. His other hand came to rest on my cheek, his eyes boring down into mine with an unrecognisable emotion. Every so slowly, his lips depended to mine. My eyes fell shut as they pressed gently on mine. I wasn't sure if I would ever get used to the feeling of butterflies in my stomach, my mind swimming with ecstasy as his fingers rubbed against my jaw.

He pulled away slowly, eyeing me with intensity as he sighed.

"Roux," he whispered huskily. "I-"

His phone ringing from the bench top had us both pulling away quickly. His eyes darted from the phone to mine, as if debating whether or not to answer it. He looked angry, walking quickly to the bench as he huffed.

"It's the firm," he mumbled. "I'm sorry." He sighed, answering the phone and walking out of the room as if nothing had happened.

CHAPTER 28

Declan didn't come out of his office that night, and I was forced to go to bed without speaking to him. Yesterday was filled with awkward apologies and his constant arguments over the phone. He said he was speaking with work, though I had never heard a professional speak as rudely as he had been, to whoever was on the other line.

I had tried to get his attention in the brief moments he would exit his office for a coffee, to ask if he was okay, if something had happened. He had only given me tight smiles however, quickly retreating to his office when I tried to approach him. I had even tried to go in and apologise for whatever I had done last night, however, once again the door had been locked and I had given up completely, forcing my way up the stairs for an early bed.

Most of my time had been spent in the upstairs library, trying to distract my thoughts from how wrong it felt to be here without his acknowledgment. I thought perhaps he would come up to find me like he had that morning with the omelettes, yet he never did.

I wasn't sure what to think. Right when we had made a

leap in our relationship, he had become aloof. It surely couldn't just be the office, he was a lawyer he had to be used to being under pressure from them. *No, this had to be more.* This had to have something to do with me. I had to have done something to annoy him.

I had sat in the kitchen this morning, hoping he would join me for breakfast, feeling terrible for going through his pantry and settling on a banana instead of cooking. When he hadn't shown then either, I decided enough was enough. I was not going to be made stay in this house for my 'protection', when Declan couldn't even leave his office to say good morning. A hotel in the city had to be just as safe. Maybe even Quinn's, surely she would be over our disagreement by now.

So as I stood at the bed, shoving my clothes into my bags, I couldn't help but scowl at how awfully this had turned out in such a short period of time. I knew staying here if this continued though would be worse. At least if I left it may have given him some space to cool off. I didn't want whatever we had, to be ruined because of something that he couldn't even talk to me about. Especially when I had been trying to talk to him about it for twenty four hours and he had yet to utter a word to me. With the rest of the stress in my life right now, I didn't need to worry about this as well.

Taking one last look at the room around me I rolled my eyes. He just needed to cool down, then we'd be fine and we could go back to how things were. I contemplated leaving without even trying to tell him, as I made my way down the stairs. As I walked past his office door though, I knew I would feel terrible later for not trying, so I banged as hard as I could in hopes that he would get the message that it was important. I allowed him about ten seconds, before my body contorted in anger again and I rolled my eyes, storming for the door.

"Yes?"

I spun with so much force that I almost fell over, steading myself with my bag. I couldn't help but scoff at the coffee in his hand. So he had been out of his office, just when he knew I wasn't around.

"I'm leaving," I muttered as I turned back to the door, phone in hand ready to call a taxi.

"What? No!" I ignored him, and his office door slamming closed. "What do you mean you're leaving?"

The angry tone in his voice had been enough to shred the last string of maturity that had been holding together my composure.Spinning, my hands were thrown in the air as I lost it.

"Because I'm not going to stay here like a damsel in distress while you lock yourself away in your office, acting like a child and refusing to talk to me over something that I don't even understand!"

He googled at me, as if unsure of what to do next. His silence was all the confirmation I needed as I spun on my heel, ready to get the hell out of this house and as far away from him as I could.

I was spun quickly, his soft grip on my wrist pulling me closer as his bloodshot eyes met mine. When I looked closer at his face, I realised just how wrecked he looked. It was as if he had gotten no sleep at all.

"I'm sorry," he whispered, his forehead coming to rest on mine as his eyes fell shut.

I couldn't help it as my shoulders slump, my body half falling into him as his lips pecked my cheek.

"I've had to deal with something, I wasn't trying to avoid you."

"What something?" I asked tiredly, my bag slipping from my shoulder to the floor.

"It's a work thing, Roux," he grumbled. "I can't tell you."

I slowly pulled away, eyeing him and the sincerity in his eyes. I knew he couldn't speak with me about his work, I knew there was confidentiality involved but I also didn't want him to avoid me like a bad smell every time he got a call.

"Okay."

A slight smile came over his face.

"Are we okay?" he asked softly.

"Yes," I whispered, leaning up to place a small kiss, on his chapped lips. "No more avoiding me."

He was nodding before I had even finished my sentence, pulling me into a hug as his fingers tangled in my hair, massaging my scalp in a way that had my knees wobbling like jelly.

"Come on, I'll cook you breakfast," he smiled cheekily, pulling my arm as he dragged me to the kitchen, my bags being deserted at the door.

"It's okay if you have to work, Declan, I don't want you trapped here with me while all of this is going on just because you think I need a babysitter, you just need to talk to me sometimes."

"No, no," he brushed me off, lifting my waist to sit me on one of the stools as if I was a toddler. "I already told the firm I was working from home for the next few days, and I need a break from my office anyway."

He was too busy pulling ingredients from the fridge to notice my eye-roll, the butter and milk sliding along the bench as he threw them onto it. I had assumed he was making another omelette, however, as he pulled the berries from the fridge I gave him a quizzical look. I knew he was a good cook, but surely this combination had to be a little unappetising.

"Pancakes?" he said questioningly, to the odd look I was

giving him and I couldn't stop the short bark of laughter that escaped my lips.

"Oh, okay."

He simply gave me a funny look and went back to collecting some more things from the pantry. He pulled out the mixing bowl and a whisk, wiggling his eyebrows at me as he cracked the first egg.

"Do you need any help?"

His smirk was enough to make my feet fall down to the ground as I jumped off the stool, not bothering to wait for his answer.

"You could measure out the milk," he nodded towards the jug and cup. "We only need one cup, then two of the flour if you don't mind."

Pouring the milk from the fancy looking jug was easier said than done as I spilt some on the bench, trying to find a hand towel or something quickly while his back was turned as he grabbed the frying pan. He turned quickly through, eyeing me curiously as I stood straight, my body concealing the mess I had made on the bench.

"What are you doing?" he asked, smirking oddly at my rigid stance.

What on earth was I meant to do now. I let my shoulders fall as I frowned, moving away from the bench to reveal the milk splatters over the marble.

"Miss Fallon," he scolded sarcastically, shaking his head as he pulled open a drawer and pulled out the paper towel. "Trying to hide the mess you made, how dare you," he joked, his voice turning into a posh accent at the end. Rolling my eyes, I took the paper towel, trying to wipe up the spill.

"It's not my fault you have a weird jug," I muttered under my breath.

"What?" he asked, poring the flour into the measuring cup.

"Nothing."

"I'm sorry?" he asked sarcastically as he eyed me with a grin. "Would you care to repeat that?"

Before I could make my legs move, the flour hit my face like an explosion, covering me in white as I coughed and spluttered.

"Declan!"

I couldn't see him as I swung my arms out to hit him, but I could hear his booming laughter as he moved around the kitchen.

"You're so dead."

"Only if you can catch me." He laughed, his breath right next to my ear. I gripped him quickly, a small seal coming from his lips as our feet tangled and we both fell to the floor. My breath hitched for a moment, as we tumbled down, though the wooden floorboards seemed to catch us much more gracefully than I had imagined, the both of us landing in a fit of laughter as we clung to each other.

"You're a butthole," I hiccupped out, my breath catching as I sucked in more flour.

"A funny butthole."

He twisted in such a manner that he was on top of me, one arm pressed out beside me to support his weight as his fingers gently wiped my eyes of the flour.

"Better?"

I smiled, my fingers gripping a handful of the powder that had fallen to the floor, before I quickly ran my fingers through his hair.

"Better."

CHAPTER 29

I ate my pancakes in silence at the table. Declan sat across from me, scoffing his portion down as if there was no tomorrow. My stomach ached from laughing, and my cheeks hurt from the amount that I had been smiling this morning. Considering how it had started, I would say that today had been a great success.

It was surprisingly sunny today, an oddity for the winter months in the city, the air still cold, however, the breeze blew softly through the opened windows. Declan's hair, which seemed to have grown even longer in the time that I had known him, ruffled as the wind hit it, sending strands flying behind his back as he ate. In the short time that I had been here, his beard had to have doubled in length and I found myself wondering just how many times a month he must have had to shave it.

"We should watch a movie today, I feel like a bit of relaxing might do us both good, tomorrow we could go into the town for a look if you like?" he asked through his mouthful of food.

A movie, I thought. I hadn't watched a movie in weeks.

Although, I hadn't had the chance to properly hang out with Quinn in weeks either and it was usually the two of us who would sit down and watch something together.

"Sure."

I felt a little bad, he obviously had work to do. I didn't mean to make him feel like he couldn't go and do it, I just wanted him to stop ignoring me.

"What are you thinking about in that pretty little head of yours?"

"I'm sorry for making you miss work," I grumbled, shoving another fork full in my mouth as I tried not to look at him.

"I'm going back next week, Roux, and I'm technically working from home anyway." He laughed. "I'm not bothered by staying here and getting to spend time with you. I just want to make sure you're comfortable here before I leave you on your own."

I did feel a little relieved knowing that he was going back in a few days. It definitely made me feel better about the whole situation.

"Okay, on Monday?"

"On Monday." He laughed.

His phone ringing from the bench top had us both snapping our gazes to it. His eyes fell back to mine though as he sheepishly stood from his seat to see who was calling. I knew who it was, when his brows furrowed and he got that serious look that I had only seen several times on his face.

"It's Derek."

I walked over to him quickly, surely they wouldn't have found anything this fast.

"Derek?" Declan answered, putting him on speaker as he sat his phone on the bench. "What did you find?"

Derek's long sigh came from the other end of the line.

"We managed to pull some prints from the photos and

envelope, they were already in our system, so it wasn't too hard."

So whoever had done this had been put in their system before? Who the heck was I dealing with?

"It was a male, goes to the university with Roux. Zachary Williams, we've had to bring him in a few times before."

Oh my God. Declan swallowed harshly, eyes seeming to widen at the name. I gripped the bench quickly, my mind growing dizzy as I tried to process the information. He wouldn't. It was Zach. It didn't make any sense, those pictures went back way further than our argument. There was no way that he was taking them this whole time. Not while we were still a thing.

"Roux?" Declan's arms quickly came around me as he held me steady. "You know him, don't you?"

I swallowed, nodding my head numbly as I buried my face in his chest. *Yes I knew him. I had slept with him!*

"Dec?" Derek asked.

"Yeah, yeah I'm here. Thanks man, I'll talk to you more about the whole thing later regarding how to proceed."

"Okay, all good, talk to you then."

As soon as the phone had been hung up, my feet were no longer touching the ground, instead wrapped securely around Declan's waist as he walked us both out of the kitchen towards the lounge area. He sunk into the lounge, not saying anything as he rubbed my back soothingly, his other hand entangled in my hair as I buried my face into his chest. I wasn't upset, not in the way that I thought I would have been. I felt numb, as if a part of me had completely shut off with the news. Whatever I had been expecting. It wasn't that.

"Who is he?" he asked softly.

I had no idea how to even explain who he was to me. It

wasn't as if I had felt anything for him but I definitely thought we knew each other a lot better than this.

"I slept with him a few times," I answered honestly. "We weren't super close…I didn't think he'd do anything like this."

Derek had said that the prints were already in their system. So Zach had been arrested before? That didn't make any sense. Zach may have been a hot head, however the whole time that I had known him the worst thing he had ever done was skip class to go and smoke with the stoners. Surely there had to be something else going on here. Maybe there had been a mistake?

"Here," Declan mumbled, pushing me off him and onto the lounge gently. "I'll go and make you a coffee, you have to tell me what you want Derek to do."

He slid off the lounge, hurrying back to the kitchen. How was I ever meant to decide what to do with Zach? I felt like I couldn't make a decision without talking to him but I didn't want to talk to him about any of this. I didn't want to put him in a position where he was arrested for something as silly as this, though my stomach also was churning with the thought that this may not have been such a silly thing. He had taken photos of me without me knowing. Of me with Declan. *Oh gosh, he had known about Declan?* Yet he still got so angry when I had broken things off. This whole thing was so confusing.

The smell of the coffee seemed to stimulate the dull ache in my head into a raging, pulsing pain. My eyes fell shut, trying to subdue it. I hadn't had a coffee in days, I was probably going through a caffeine withdrawal or something equally as stupid. *Or it could be because I just found out that Zach is a full-on stalker*, I thought. *Yep. That's probably it.*

"Here."

My eyes opened to a steaming mug in front of my face. I took it gladly, knowing that it would ease my jitters if only slightly. The first gulp was enough to have a short moan slim out. *I missed you, my friend.* Declan sat beside me, his own cup in his hand as he slipped the blanket off of the back of the lounge, pulling it over the both of us.

"Do you want to talk about it?" he asked.

I shook my head quickly.

"Not just yet, later."

He nodded, grabbing the remote and rubbing my leg comfortingly.

An hour or so later, I was comfortably spread across the lounge, my legs hanging over him as we watched whatever the movie was he had put on. It was only mid-day, yet my eyes were begging me to close them and let sleep take over. I refused though, knowing that I would wake up feeling worse if I let myself fall asleep now. Declan's eyes bounced from the TV to me frequently enough for me to know that it wasn't just a casual glance. He was obviously worried about, maybe that I was going to have a mental breakdown or something. He didn't need to be though. Whilst the news of Zach had upset me, I was glad that it was him and not someone like Will, which would have made my life more than complicated. Zach sucked. That much I was sure of. He was an utter slime ball and if I ever got the chance I would gladly punch him in the face.

Another thing, I missed Quinn. I wanted to call her more than anything and explain everything that had happened. Let her know that my life had turned into a reality tv show and that she needed to hurry up and get her butt back here to be the supportive best friend I needed. She would know what to do in this situation. Her life was one big ball dramatics and I was sure that she would be able to walk into this situation and play the role of Roux Fallon much better than I was.

"How are you feeling?"

Declan's question pulled me from my thoughts as our eyes met.

"Better."

He nodded, shifting so that I was cradled in his lap.

"Want to talk about it yet?"

I wasn't sure as I buried my face into his chest. I wasn't even sure what I thought about it, let alone act to say.

"Did you like him, the guy?" he asked softly.

I laughed a little, raising an eyebrow at his question.

"No. We weren't together like that. I'm not hurt by what he did, just annoyed that he did it."

"Oh, okay."

"Can we talk about something else? Anything?" I asked. "I'm fine, really, let's just change the subject."

He eyed me for a moment before he nodded.

"I would like to take you on a date in the morning," he said, spinning me so that I was sitting, facing him in his lap.

"A date?"

He nodded, biting his lip as he pressed his forehead to mine.

"As my girlfriend."

My spine went rigid, eyes widening as I opened my mouth only to snap it shut moments later. Declan's face seemed to slowly fall as his eyes grew.

"No, no!" I laughed. "I mean well, yes. I would love that."

"Really?" His smile was back.

"Yes!" I shouted, leaning down to smash my lips on his. He reacted quickly, his arms wrapping around me quickly as he laughed into the kiss. I pulled back just as quickly, raking in his face.

How had I gotten so lucky?

"Thank you," I whispered, pecking his lips again.

"For what?" he murmured, his lips trying to find mine again.

"For the distraction," I said sincerely.

He pulled back slowly, his mouth lifting up as his soft hands found their way into my own, entwining with my fingers.

"I've been wanting to ask you that since you told me that it was up to me to clarify the relationship," he mumbled, placing a soft kiss to my forehead. "It was definitely not just a distraction."

I had no idea what to say. Nothing came to my mind on how on earth to respond to such a thing. So instead, I let my lips fall back on his, savouring the moment as I kissed him softly.

CHAPTER 30

The cold weather seemed to be back when I opened my eyes the next morning, the only thing that had been keeping me warm was Declan who had laid underneath me. Both us having fallen asleep on the lounge last night, the afternoon having been spent watching movies and laughing at each other. A smile came to my face at the memory of trying to catch grapes in my mouth that Declan had insisted on throwing. Of course, he had tried to sneak away about half an hour ago, slipping out from under me carefully, as I faked being asleep.

Even if he hadn't, I could hear him singing ridiculously as the shower ran somewhere on the second floor above me. I was sure he would have woken me with the racket anyway. His room must have been close to mine, I realised. There hadn't been too many bedrooms on the second floor. The sound of the water turning off and his soft singing dulling down to a hum, had me clutching my belly as I tried to laugh as quietly as possible. *Who on earth was I dating?* I jumped a little, opening my mouth at my own thought as I rolled around more. I could say that now! We were dating! Oh my gosh, my stomach felt like it was on a slippery dip, my cheeks aching from the ridiculous grin I couldn't wipe off my face.

"Good morning, gorgeous."

I jumped, turning to look at Declan who stood on the steps in a pair of jeans, no shirt covering his upper half as I tried not to ogle at his muscles.

"Good morning."

With a view like this, I thought, *what a fantastic morning it was.*

"Aren't you going to get ready for our date?" He smirked.

Our date. The town. Oh gosh. I tried not to look sheepish as I threw the blanket off me, running past him as I made my way up the stairs. His hands reached for me as I ran, a squeal slipping through my lips as I dodged him.

"I'd hurry if I were you!" he called. "The diner has the best breakfast but it stops serving in an hour!"

An hour? I could be ready in ten minutes. I showered quicker than I ever had before, jumping out and throwing on my usual turtleneck and paper-bag pants, grabbing a coat as I ran back down the stairs, throwing my hair up into a low bun on the way.

Declan, who seemed to be tying his shoes, looked at me as if he had seen a ghost.

"I'm ready." I breathed, trying not to seem as unfit as I was.

"That was quick."

I waved him off, grabbing my phone from the bench and shrugging as I pecked him on the cheek.

"Let's do this!" I cheered, grabbing his arm as he shook his head in laughter, leading me to the door.

"You really are something, Rouxette Fallon."

I almost scoffed at him.

"Never call me Rouxette," I said, staring into his eyes as seriously as I could. "I hate it."

"Why?"

"It makes me sound like a grandma," I grumbled, slipping my hand into his as he pulled me onto a path that led around the lake.

"You're silly."

"I prefer unique," I joked.

The path enclosed us with thick trees the further we walked. I could hear the distant sounds of people talking, children laughing. It was odd to be able to hear voices instead of traffic, however reminded me of my hometown in a way that had me quickening my steps to see exactly what it looked like.

As the trees slipped away and the path came to a stop, I realised we were in a park. The playground in front of us was covered in laughing children as their parents watched on from the bench seats.

"Over there is the diner," he pointed, the corner building looking busy with the amount of people that sat around the tables outside.

"It looks a bit busy."

"Ha, don't worry about that, there's always room." He laughed.

I didn't bother arguing as he pulled us past the park, across the road and towards the small diner. The smell that wafted out from within it was delicious and had my mouth watering with hunger that I didn't even realise I had been feeling.

"The town isn't very big, this is the only diner, it's usually pretty full."

"I should take you to my hometown sometime," I smiled. "You would be surprised at how small I'm used to."

"You in a small town?" He smirked. "I can't picture it."

My mouth dropped in offence, however, I was cut off as Declan opened the door to the diner, a hush seeming to fall over the crowd inside as they tried to hide their curious gazes.

"Marcelo!" A man wearing an apron yelled, as he hung his head out from the doorway to the kitchen, giving us both a cheeky grin as he waved a spatula around. "Who have you brought with you?" he asked happily, a surprised look crossing his face as his eyes came to settle on mine.

Declan looked down at me, a small blush covering his cheeks as he rolled his eyes at the man.

"This is Roux," he said, wrapping an arm around my shoulders. "I don't suppose you have a table for two left?"

I looked around the restaurant, there didn't seem to be a free table in sight.

"Oh, for you my boy, of course! Try out the back, the usual should be free." He laughed, as if he had told a joke. Declan just shook his head with a smile, pulling me along as he walked to the back of the diner, opening a small door and pushing me out. Outside was beautiful. The small back section of the diner seemed to only have two tables, both empty and sitting on bright green grass, surrounded by flowers. I had no idea why no one would be sitting out here, it seemed to be the best spot in the whole place.

"Okay so my father and I may have used to come here a lot," he mumbled sheepishly as he pulled a chair out for me. "We would always come and sit out here, my mother used to joke that we were a pair of garden gnomes, sitting out here all day smelling the flowers." He laughed. "They don't usually let people sit out here anymore, I guess I'm the exception."

The back door swung open to reveal a young girl, probably around sixteen, who wore an apron and carried a notepad over to us.

"Hi ya'll! What can we get for you this morning?"

I looked wide eyed down at the table, confused with the lack of menu.

"We'll have two of the chef's specials thank you," Declan replied. "With a long black and a cappuccino."

She wrote down our order quickly, giving us both a big grin.

"Is that all?"

"Yes, thank you," he answered.

She nodded once again and turned to walk quickly back into the diner. Declan eyed the door before turning to me.

"She's new," he said simply, raising an eyebrow as he folded his arms. "Business must be getting bigger than usual for Ben to bring in more staff." He smiled, seeing my odd look. "Sorry, I just mean I'm glad that it's going well." He blushed, looking down at the flowers on the ground.

"How long have you lived at the lake house?" I asked.

"Ever since I can remember I guess." He shrugged. "My father built it before I was born, they only moved to Europe a few years ago. That was why I originally brought my apartment in the city, more freedom when I started university. When they moved though and my father offered it to me, I knew I couldn't turn it down."

"Wow, I thought you must have moved here or something."

"Nope," he answered simply, leaning down to pick a flower from the ground.

"For you," he said, leaning over to place it behind my ear. I pursed my lips, trying not to smile at his antics.

"Smooth."

He nodded, biting his lip to stop the laughter that had started bubbling out.

"Smooth as butter, baby."

The door opening again had our laughter stopping short as we tried not to look like complete teenagers in front of the waitress, who held out coffees in her hand.

"The cappuccino," she said softly, putting it in front of

Declan, before placing mine on the table beside it. "And the long black." She smiled. "Your meals should be ready soon, the chef said to tell you that he's rushing them through now."

"Great," Declan grinned, eyeing my confusion with humour. "What can I say? I'm his favourite."

I rolled my eyes, sitting back in my seat and waiting for our food to come out.

The food had been delicious and by the time we had finished Declan insisted that we beat the rain and head home quickly, having forgotten an umbrella.

"Oh my goodness," I snickered sarcastically, walking along the path with him. "Declan Marcelo actually forgetting something?"

"Oh stop it."

Before I knew what was happening, I had been pushed unexpectedly, my legs giving out from under me as I toppled over sideways into a spiky bush. I sucked in a hard breath as I felt the thorns break the skin of my arm.

"Oh God, Roux!"

I was ripped out of the bush quickly, my eyes watering as my arm stung. Looking down, I could see the small trickles of blood running from the cuts. It wasn't as bad as it had felt like.

"I'm so sorry," he whispered, lifting me easily from the ground as my legs wrapped around his waist.

"Declan, it's fine," I mumbled, trying to avoid the blood running onto his shirt. "And I can walk."

"No, I'm really sorry Roux, I didn't realise there was a bush there, I swear."

"Declan, it's just a scratch."

He shook his head, moving faster towards the house, the short walk becoming even quicker with his long strides. As we broke through the end of the path that led to the house, I tried to shimmy my way down. Declan didn't let go however, his grip on my lower back tightening as he held me closer to him.

He was silent as he walked us both up the steps to the front door, opening it quickly before moving his way up the stairs into a bedroom that I had seen that first day here. The ensuite attached was large as he pushed the door open and walked me in. I finally sat down on the sink, his movements frantic as he searched through the cupboards, finding a small red bag under the sink, in between my legs.

"Here," he mumbled slowly, pulling a small alcohol wipe and gauze from the pack.

"Declan..." I laughed, rolling my eyes at the supplies. "It's fine, the gauze is a bit unnecessary."

He didn't listen though, his own eyes rolling at my words as he held my arm gently, lifting it so that he could get a closer look. He ripped the alcohol wipe packet open with his teeth, eyeing me intently as he did so. It stung as he smoothed it across the cuts and I hissed as I tried to ignore the pain.

"See," he mumbled smugly. "It needed a clean."

I ignored him, the cuts still burning. As he placed the soft gauze on my arm though, they seemed to calm down, turning more into a light itch.

Sighing, he threw the kit back under the bench. Eyeing me from below my legs.

"I'm sorry."

"Declan, stop apologising," I said sternly. "It was nothing."

He was up, lifting me from the sink in seconds, as my legs wrapped around his waist once again.

"It might be nothing to you Roux, but it is something for me. I don't want to ever hurt you, accidentally or on purpose."

The intensity in his eyes had my cheeks heating with his sweet words, his lips quickly coming to attack mine, with a gentle force. I matched his actions, kissing him back with equal force, as my back came to gently rest on the bathroom wall. *Why did his kisses have to feel so good? Why did he have to feel so good?*

"Roux," he whispered, his eyes looking down into mine as he pulled back from the kiss.

"Please," I said softly, answering his unasked question. His lips were back on mine in a second, kissing with more force than they ever had before. I hardly noticed when the bathroom door had opened, when he had laid me back softly on the bed.

All I seemed to be able to think about was how amazing this man on top of me was.

CHAPTER 31

*D*eclan's fingers ran through my hair as he scrubbed the shampoo into my scalp. The warm water from the shower left my cold body rippling with goosebumps, his soft fingers not helping as they tickled my neck.

"I have to go back to work tomorrow," he mumbled against my neck and I found myself falling down from the high I had been riding.

"Tomorrow?"

It was already nearly nightfall, I couldn't believe how quickly the week had flown by.

"I'll be a phone call away if anything happens, and you can always go into town and have a look around if you like."

I wasn't even worried that anything could happen, I was more so down about the fact that I wasn't going to be able to spend my free time with him anymore. Of course, this did have one benefit, being that I would actually be able to get some of my work done if he wasn't around to distract me. Although I hadn't seemed to do any work within the last week or so, I was surprised when I received my online assignments, which I wasn't behind on at all. I just had to hope it was because I had submitted my others early and not because Declan had anything to do with it.

"I'll miss you," he whispered, his lips pressing gently to my cheek.

"I'll miss you too." I laughed lightly.

"Have you made a decision on how you want to proceed with Zach? I'll probably get a call from Derek soon about it."

Now that was a question that I had no idea how to answer. In simple terms, no. I hadn't made a decision about anything regarding what happened. I knew what I wanted to do. I wanted to tell them to go and arrest him right then and there. I wanted to know that I was safe and that I could leave and go back to my dorm and see Quinn and Will. In all honesty though, I felt terrible for thinking like that. I knew he probably deserved it. I understood that what he did was terrible, I just needed to make sure that I was okay with completely ruining someone's life. Especially Zach's.

"Can I decide in the morning?"

"Of course," he mumbled, his lips finding their way to my neck as he trailed a line of soft kisses across my shoulder. "Take all the time you need."

"Thank you."

His soft hands slowly spun me around and pulled me under the water with him. I snapped my eyes shut as the water hit my hair, the shampoo slowly trickling down my face as he massaged it out. His fingers were like magic as they worked their way around my scalp, seeming to rid me of all my worries and tension, allowing every muscle in my body to relax. Tumbling from my lips came a soft sigh as I allowed myself to fall into him, his arms wrapping securely around me as he held me close under the water.

"How did I get this lucky?"

His words had my eyes snapping open regardless of the

shampoo, our eyes meeting as a slow smile fell upon his lips. The best part was, I was thinking the exact same thing.

The next morning rolled around quickly, Declan's bed having been much more comfortable than the one in the spare room.

"I'll be back before you know it," Declan chuckled, trying to reason with me as I clung to him at the front door. His tie was tightly gripped in my hand as he grinned down at me, shaking his head as he took a step forward, swooping down to meet my lips quickly.

"Roux," he groaned. "You're making it difficult to leave."

Sighing, I released him, taking another step forward to quickly place a kiss to his cheek.

"I'm sorry, I'm just going to miss you," I whispered sheepishly.

"I'm going to miss you too, I'll be home by…" his eyes widened as he looked down at his wrist, his eyes scanning the small room before he quickly walked to his office door fiddling with the lock before he stuck a hand in and pulled it out, revealing his watch.

"I almost forgot." He laughed. "But three, I should be home by three."

I let him walk to the door then. Three wasn't that bad. Three was reasonable. I needed to study anyway.

"We can watch another movie tonight if you like? You can pick," he winked, quickly stepping out of the door, and giving me a small wave. "Have fun!" he called.

"You too!"

The door shut quickly behind him.

Okay, I thought. *Time to catch up on some work.*

Twenty minutes later I was looking at my laptop screen, scowling as I reread the second line of my essay. It was terrible. Utter B.S and it was probably so bad because the only thing running through my head was the realisation that, I needed to come to a decision about Zach. Today. I needed to decide whether or not I wanted to press charges and I still had no idea. *I would figure it out before Declan came home*, I thought. For now distraction through studying would have to be enough.

As I worked my way through however, pulling my notebook out ready to take notes, I realised that I didn't have a pen. *Surely Declan had one somewhere*, I thought. He's a lawyer for trying out loud. The real question though, was where? I made my way into the main room quickly, walking to the buffet drawers and the TV unit, opening the drawers and scouring for anything that I could use to write with. Everything came up empty however, so I made my way to the kitchen, opening the kitchen cupboards and searching through, with still no luck. It was then, as I was closing the last draw and losing hope that I realised how foolish I was. *The reading room*, I thought. The desk there would surely have to have a pen, pencil or really anything that I could use.

As I was about to walk up the stairs however, my eyes were drawn to the left. The door to Declan's office was open a sliver, as if almost taunting me with the unfamiliarity. Well, he had to have a pen in there, it was an office...

The room was smaller than I had imagined, darker too as I tried to see my way in the little light. I could make out faintly the string of a light cord hanging from the ceiling and I tried not to laugh at the outdated manner of it. As I pulled it, the click allowed it to slowly flicker to light up the room. Each pulse seemed to grow brighter until I could make out the small desk in front of me. There seemed to be paper everywhere, piles upon piles of files and paperwork stacked as high as my knees.

My eyes caught on a picture that was pinned to the wall, held tightly with a thumbtack and red coloured string that ran across another. That-That was me? As I moved closer to get a better look, I realised that the one it was connected to, was also of me...and the next and the one after that. My eyes widened, my heart starting to race in my chest as I ran my gaze over the whole room. It was all me. Quinn and I. Me and Will. Zach. All strung together by coloured wool that seemed to create a spider web collection of my life across the room. *Oh my gosh. What the fuck?* What. The. Fuck. They were everywhere, pinned wherever they seemed to fit. Pictures of everything. Coffee dates with Quinn, walking to my lectures, laughing with Will.

One yellow string led to a picture of my broken dorm room door. The word *close* etched underneath on a sticky note. Another, from one of my first days that I had been on campus. It had been taken so long ago that the edges of the picture had started to wear.

I couldn't breathe. My lungs closed in on themselves as I looked down at the desk. Every piece of paperwork seems to have my picture or name on it. My school records. University ID's. The most eye-catching was the yellow notepad, which seemed to have a short list of names on it. Mine being highlighted in a bright purple. *Safe List*, it was labelled. I couldn't seem to pull in any air. Nothing about this was safe. My chest was on fire. My eyes burning with unleashed tears. *No. No.* I wanted to cry. This couldn't be happening!

I stepped back, the feeling of something crunching under my feet had a short, scared breath sucked into my mouth. A shattered red pen sat bleeding onto the floor. The red ink seemed to spark a false in my mind as my feet gradually hurried backwards, picking up pace until I had slammed the office door closed, hysteria taking over as I screamed a sob that had been building in my chest.

The tears didn't stop falling as I ran up the stairs and grabbed my phone. The sobs didn't stop wracking my body as I ran as fast as I could, my breath hitching with every step, dialling one of the only numbers that I knew by heart.

I held it to my ear, tripping slightly down the stairs, my shin erupting in fire as I tied to hobble to the front door. The ringing continued as I fumbled with the old lock, my shaking hands struggling to grip the small handle.

"Hi," Quinn's soft breath came from the other end of the phone.

"Quinn!" I hiccupped.

My heart raced. Head dizzy. Ears pounding with my quick pulse.

"Roux?" she asked.

"Please," I begged. "Please come get me, I can't, he, he-" I tried to catch my breath as I cried, my fingers finally moving the small lock enough that I threw the door open, the cold wet wind slapping against my face as I ran out of the house.

"What happened?" her voice was calm, yet scary, as if she was already plotting to bury someone.

"Come get me," I cried. "I'm in a town not far from the city, half an hour max."

I was surprised she understood my blubbering words, as I fumbled my way down the familiar path that gave way to the park. The harsh rain slapped against my face as I ran, stinging as I pushed further.

"I'm on my way."

I could hear a jingle of keys, a door slamming.

"What's it called?" she asked.

"I don't know Quinn! I never asked!" I sobbed. "Hang on."

The park was up ahead and the park was in the town. The name had to be plastered somewhere.

I must have looked like a corpse as I stumbled into the abandoned park, everyone having left due to the weather. My eyes caught the familiar diner and I found my chest clenching at the thought of how nice it had been. How nice

Declan had been. Then I realised. The name. Lake Earnest Diner. *Oh my gosh.*

"Lake Earnest?" I hoped, Quinn's fingers tapping wildly on the screen.

"I got it! Stay on the phone with me! I'll be there in twenty."

"I'm so sorry, Quinn," I sobbed, making my way underneath the shelter of the shaded area. The wind still slapped against my back like a cold whip, however at least the rain couldn't drench me further.

"I know," her voice cracked. "But now is not the time, Roux, where are you? What building?"

"I'm in the park."

"Roux, it's freezing!" she yelled, a car horn in the background causing a curse to fall from her lips.

"Trust me," I gulped. "I'd rather be here."

"Just hang on, I'm coming."

CHAPTER 32

Quinn's bubble car tore around the corner, skidding slightly in the rain as she came to an abrupt stop, swinging the door open before she had put it in park. I was already running, my legs burning with the cold as I cried harder in the unshielded rain, diving into the passenger seat and swinging my door closed. Quinn didn't wait for an explanation, taking off just as fast as she had pulled up as she eyed me with horror.

"What the fuck happened?"

"His office. It's filled with pictures of me, of us," I cried. "There's everything, Quinn! I mean it's full of information on me! My pictures, my school records, everything!"

"Oh my God. How did you get in his office?" She asked, her voice wavering.

Oh gosh. She had no idea about anything!

"Zach, he was stalking me, he, he had all these pictures," I gasped. "But maybe it wasn't him! Maybe it was Declan! Oh my gosh! I don't know anymore!" I cried.

"Roux, calm down, explain it to me, calmly."

I drew in a quick breath, her car zooming out of the town quickly.

"I was staying with Declan being Zach had been stalking my old dorm, then when Declan went to work this morning I looked for a pen in his office. He had it locked all the other times, I didn't even think about why. When I went in though, oh gosh, Quinn. He's a psycho."

"We need to call the police."

"NO!" I yelled quickly. "He's brother! He's a cop, oh gosh, he's probably in on it! We can't, he'll find out where we are!"

She looked frantic for a moment, the same hysteria on my face seeming to slowly make its way to hers.

"Shit!" she whispered, "Well, we have to go somewhere, what about my dorm?"

"He had pictures of you strung up on his wall, Quinn! I think I know where he's going to look first!"

She was panicking now. Her eyes widening as her breathing became uneven.

"A hotel?"

"Yeah," I nodded. "That sounds good."

"His brother can't be the only cop in the city," she reasoned.

My stomach churned as I thought back to that first morning I saw him in the alley way.

"It doesn't mean he is the only one in on it."

She screamed then, her fist hitting the steering wheel as a tear escaped her eye.

"Fuck! We need to get a hotel and think about what to do next," she said sternly. "We're going to the police, we just need to plan this out."

I nodded, my sobs turning into small hiccups as I turned my head to watch out the window. The roads slowly grew larger as the buildings grew into the city.

"How could I be so stupid?" I whispered, my eyes falling shut to stop the tsunami that was raging in my eyes.

I should have known it was too good to be true. But his office. Oh my gosh. I had never seen something so unsettling in my life. I couldn't believe I was on display, my whole life, for him to string up and search. The nights he had spent locked away in his office…oh gosh. I didn't want to think about what he had been doing.

Why? Why me? He already had me, why did he need to do that?

My phone started buzzing, Declan's name flashing across the screen as I sucked in a breath. He couldn't be home. It wasn't three. He couldn't have even finished yet.

"Is it him?" she asked, I could tell she was trying to act as if she didn't care, but the waver in her voice told me otherwise.

"Yeah."

"You need to ditch that phone."

"What?"

"You said his brother is a cop? He can probably track your phone, you should get rid of it," she clarified.

I looked down at it in my hands, frowning as our eyes met.

"But-"

"You can always get a new one, Roux."

I tried not to watch as I slowly rolled down the window, more tears forming in my eyes as I let my hand hang for a moment, slowly opening it as the wind snatched up my phone, spiralling it far away from us.

"What about yours?"

She seemed to think for a moment before her face broke into a frown. She shimmied her hips, grabbing the phone from her jean pocket before she glared at me.

"We better not die, because if I waste my phone for no reason I'm going to kill you."

Then it was gone out her open window as if it was nothing but a leaf.

"I love you," I muttered, the tears slowly coming to a stop the further from the town and house that we drove.

"You better."

A few hours later, we were sitting in the shabby hotel room on the far side of the city. We had yet to come up with a plan, my eyes sore from crying and Quinn's face having turned red and splotchy.

"We need to go to your dorm," she muttered from beside me on the bed.

"Are you crazy?"

"We need to see if we can find anything else to take to the cops when we figure out a plan, maybe ask the desk lady if anyone has been to your dorm in the past few days?"

Okay that made a little bit of sense.

"What if something happens?"

She rolled her eyes, looking at me as if I was stupid.

"Something has already happened and I highly doubt he would cause a scene in a populated dorm building, especially not when we're both there and help is only a scream away."

She had a point, I still don't feel great about any of it though.

"When do you want to do this?"

"In the morning. I think we should sleep now, clear our heads. We don't want to have to deal with this while we're still not thinking clearly. We're safe here, let's just be safe for now."

"Okay," I whispered, laying down as Quinn did. We both didn't speak, just slithered under the thin blanket and curled up next to each other, trying to get some extra warmth.

My gosh, I had missed Quinn. My heart was yearning for her even now and I was beside her. Declan had seemed to take up all space in my mind when I was around him, leaving me unable to mourn the loss of friendship that I had experienced. The thought of Declan was another whole that dug deep within me. I had truly thought he was an amazing person. The way he had made me feel was unmatched by anyone else I had ever been interested in. I thought perhaps, just maybe, we could have become soothing more. That we may have been able to last.

Tears formed in my eyes as I frowned deeply. I was wrong. We weren't meant to last. Everything had been a lie. A scheme to get closer to me, to draw me in. I didn't want to think about what would have happened if I had stayed there longer.

I was just happy to be here, with Quinn and the echo in my hurting soul.

Morning came too quickly, half the night being spent twisting and turning, the other half in breath-taking nightmares. By the time that Quinn had rolled her way out of bed, throwing the covers off and demanding that I 'hurry my ass up and get dressed', I felt worse than I had the day before.

"You look like shit," she tried to joke, throwing me my coat from the chair.

"Can you blame me?"

Her smirk disappeared as she pulled me in for a stiff hug.

"Were going to sort this out and you're not going to have to see him again, okay?"

I nodded, my face buried in her neck that smelt of her expensive perfume.

"Get sorted," she muttered softly, "I'll go get the car warm, we can't waste anymore time."

"Okay."

She didn't stick around, walking briskly out into the cold morning air and leaving me in the small room by myself. When I was alone. It was a little easier to think. My thoughts rushing to the surface, as well as my emotions. I wanted to open my eyes and have this all be some sick dream. Declan's arms wrapped tightly around me in his comfortable bed as he offered to go and make pancakes. No matter how many times I closed and opened my eyes though, I still saw the same room.

I gathered my socks and shoes slowly, taking my time in putting them on. I didn't feel nervous anymore for what we were about to do. I felt ready to feel safe again. I wanted this over with as quickly as possible. I still had no idea how we were going to go about the police thing but I knew that Quinn was right. Not every cop in the city was a fraud. I just had to find one who wasn't connected to Declan or Derek.

Sighing, I stood on shaky legs, looking around the room one last time before I walked out the door, down to Quinn in the car and towards freedom.

CHAPTER 33

"I figured it out," I mumbled numbly as we pulled up to the dorm parking.

"What?" Quinn asked, confused.

"Declan's brother said that they found fingerprints on the envelope that matched Zach's. Declan used Zach as an excuse to get me to move in with him. To get me closer. The pictures, everything in his office. He easily would have known that Zach and I were having issues, it was a perfect cover up."

Her breath blew out as she covered her face, shaking her head as she groaned.

"Roux, it's fucked up, we know that. The best thing you can do right now is to stop thinking about it and come inside with me.

I eyed the building with nerves, my stomach flipping at the thought of going back in.

"Do we have to?"

"Do you want answers?"

Her door was open and she was out of the car in a matter of seconds. Quinn was much more cut out for this than I ever could be. I followed suit, getting out of the car nervously as Quinn watched me with patient eyes.

"It's going to be all good, Roux," she said.

I just nodded, letting her link her arm in mine and lead me towards the door. It was warm inside, the temperature matching that of the car. It was hot enough that the administration lady sat behind the desk without a coat, her thin, long-sleeved top being much too cold for outside.

"I don't think I can do this," I heaved. I didn't want to know if anyone had been to my room win the past few days, I already knew they hadn't. Declan had been with me for days, he had no need to.

"Do you want to go look upstairs for clues, evidence?"

"This isn't a game, Quinn."

Her hand fell on my shoulder softly as she pursed her lips.

"I know you're stressed, Roux, but don't take this out on me. You should go and see if you can find anything else to pin on this bastard."

She was right. Ugh, why was she always right?

"Okay." I nodded. She smiled, pointing to the administration desk.

"I'm going to go ask questions, you go see what you can dig up."

Just as I had gained a semblance of courage, she walked away, letting it fizzle out as I eyed the stairs. *Just do it Roux. You'll thank yourself later.*

I tried not to let myself worry as I walked the familiar staircase. *It's just your dorm Roux*, I thought, pulling myself up further. *You have been in there countless times before.* I passed Will's floor, thankful that he wasn't out to question what was going on. I still had no idea what went down between him and Quinn. I wasn't even sure if we were on speaking terms at the moment.

As I made it to my floor, I tried not to let the overwhelming fear in my mind take over. *What are you scared of Roux? It's just your dorm.*

The door was still slightly ajar, where I had ran out of it carelessly last week. As I pushed it open, revealing my clean and well-presented entry way, I was surprised that no other students had spotted it and decided to sneak in. It was quiet, the only noise being my feet walking slowly on the floorboards. Everything seemed in place, as I made my way into the lounge area and I vaguely remembered Declan's business partner saying that it was a mess. Had he been lying?

My heart dropped to my stomach as I heard the door slam shut unexpectedly. I couldn't move as I heard a creak come from the entry way.

"Quinn?" I squeaked.

There was no reply and I felt the oncoming panic attack starting to eat away at my thoughts. I was paralysed, unable to scream. To move. After a few moments though, nothing happened. No noise was heard and nothing moved. *Had it been the wind?*

A hand wrapped around my throat at the same time my stomach dropped, causing my legs to give out. *It was Declan*, I thought, *I couldn't see him, but I could sense him*. I clawed at the hand, my throat burning and lungs screaming at me for air. As quickly as it had come though it was done. I sucked in a harsh breath, and then I was falling. I hit the floor with such force that the breath had been knocked out of me. I felt fingers grip my hair, before my face was thrown forwards quickly, my head pounding upon the impact with the floor.

"Please," I rasped, trying to crawl away as his fingers tightened in my hair. I saw the floor approaching again and I knew there wasn't any point in struggling. I couldn't feel as I head-butted the floorboards, my vision leaving as I was left unconscious.

The first thing I realised was that something smelt horrendously. The second, was the pounding headache that wracked my body intensely. The stench didn't help, travelling up my nose so provocatively that I felt the urge to vomit. My eyes ached, as if I had been punched in both of them. One refused to open as I tried to look round, the other a blur of grey. I needed water, air, anything that would make my throat stop aching. *What on earth happened to me?*

I had the passing thought that perhaps I needed a doctor, but I felt as though for some reason I couldn't have one.

My mind was a scrambled mess, as I tried to process what I remembered and why I was here. Wherever here was. The more I tried to think, the worse my headache grew. I had snippets flash through the fog. Declan, Quinn, my dorm. *Quinn! Oh my gosh!*

I sucked in a painful breath. Declan had gotten me. He had taken me somewhere. Kidnapped me. He was going to kill me. I only hoped that it didn't smell so badly because of any other bodies in the room.

I tried to force my eyes open, to see clearly and take in my surroundings. If I could find a way out, if I could somehow see where I was, I could escape. However, it seemed the longer I laid on the cold hard ground, the worse my eyesight grew. I tried to wipe my eyes, my arms struggling to move as I came to the panicked realisation that I was bound at both my hands and feet.

I stopped struggling as I heard movement growing closer. A dull creak filled the room, light seeming to pool in as someone opened a door. I could vaguely make out the shape of the short bulky man. He wasn't Declan. Was he his partner? Another 'worker'.

"So you're awake," it grumbled. His voice was like loose gravel as he gurgled up the words. I had never heard a more frightening voice in my life. The hair on my skin stood straight as ripples of fear coursed through me.

I tried to mutter a yes, instead a small wheeze escaped. The man just grunted.

"Rouxette Fallon," he muttered. "If only Marcelo could see you now."

I didn't want to hear about Declan, my heart race increasing more so at the mention of his name.

"You're what all this trouble is about."

"What?" I tried to ask. The hoarse wheeze squeezing out of my throat more like a donkey than a question.

"Don't act like you don't fucking know," his gruff voice grumbled.

In all honesty, I had no idea what he was talking about. Absolutely fucking none. I did know that if he didn't kill me, I was going to be taken out by fear. I shook my head, my skull pounding as another wave of pain shot through.

"You're the reason our boss is in jail."

I was sure that he had the wrong person. I had never met this man before in my life. Was his boss Declan? Surely not. Declan wasn't in jail, not yet at least.

"I, I don't know what you're talking about," my voice cracked and wheezed as I spoke, however, other than the pain it seems to come out much better than before.

I couldn't see him to take in his expression, though his silence was enough to have me shaking on the floor, my eyes snapping shut, even though I couldn't see out of them anyway.

"You're telling me," he muttered slowly. "That he kept you hidden for weeks, and you had no idea?"

None of this was making sense in my jumbled mind.

His hard grunt made me jump as I heard him stay from wherever he had been. The door leaking open harshly as his low voice filled the air.

"He just had to shoot *you*, didn't he."

The bang as the door shut had me just about jumping out of my skin, my muscles clenched tightly as the unleashed tears began to squeeze out of my swollen eyes.

What had I done to end up here?

CHAPTER 34

When my eyes finally opened again, the room was slightly clearer. I wasn't sure if I had fallen asleep or passed out, but I felt ten times worse when I woke up. The walls around me looked like cement, I was in some form of basement or underground bunker. There was only one door leading out and it seemed to be made of metal. There was no handle, no window, the only light source streaming from underneath the small crack at the bottom of the door. I almost had hope that it led outside, though the yellow light seemed to make me think that it was unlikely.

I just wanted to know why I was still here, tied up in this dark room. I was semi-convinced that this man wasn't working with Declan, from what he had mentioned before. Although, if he wasn't, then why the hell was I here? As far as I knew, I hadn't been in contact with, let alone pissed off anyone other than Declan in the past few days, really the only other contact I had aside from my mother had been Quinn and Will. They had to have the wrong person, I was sure of it. I wanted to scream, cry and plead until they could see that I had done nothing to them, that I would do nothing if they would just let me go.

As hot tears streamed down my cheeks, I realised that I was hyperventilating. My breathing quickly as my chest rose and fell. Oh my gosh. A panic attack. I was having a panic attack. My worry only grew as I realised I was having a panic attack, alone, in a small, cold cell. Surrounded by nothing but cement walls and utter regret. Regret for ever going on that run three years ago, regret for going to my study group that morning and regret for not telling Declan Marcelo to fuck off the first chance I had. I couldn't think, my mind hazy with stain as I struggled to draw in a calm breath. Everything was a mess. My head was growing heavy as I let it slowly fall to rest on the floor.

That was when I heard the door creak open once again. I didn't want to face the bulky man with seeing eyes whilst I was already having a panic attack, instead choosing to close them and hope that I passed out soon enough.

"Roux?"

My eyes snapped open as I sat up quickly, the motion making me see spots, as I felt myself fall backwards. His hands were there in a moment, holding me cautiously as he looked on with concern.

"Oh God, are you okay?"

I couldn't form a sentence as my mind went into overdrive. *What was he doing here? How did he find me? What was going on?*

"Zach?" I asked quietly.

"Here," he whispered quickly, unscrewing the cap off from a water bottle before lifting it to my lips. "Quickly, before they come back!"

I didn't waste anymore time, trying to down as much water as I could as he held the bottle. I was so thirsty, my throat cracked and raw, stinging as I downed the water. He pulled the bottle away and I found myself leaning to it and getting more.

"You'll make yourself sick, Roux."

I sobbed at his words. *Sick? I was past sick.*

"Please?" I whispered desperately, my body screaming at me for more water.

"I didn't know they were going to do this, I swear," he choked. "They just said they wanted him, they never mentioned hurting you."

"What?" I asked meekly, then I had a thought that made my whole stomach drop. "Quinn!" I gasped.

"She's fine, she wasn't in the room when they grabbed you."

"Who are they?"

Zach grimaced, eyes falling down as he shook his head.

"I'm not even meant to be here, Roux-"

"Zach it's not like it's going to matter in the end anyway just tell me who the fuck I'm being held captive by. Is it Declan? Does he have something to do with this?"

Zach looked utterly confused by my question, his forehead wrinkled as he shook his head.

"Why would...no Roux, no Declan isn't here, that's the problem. They're trying to draw him in with you."

"What?"

"Do you really not know what's going on?" he asked, eyeing me as if I had gone mad.

"No," I rushed, trying to get him to see that I was telling the truth. "I'm so confused, Zach!"

His look was pure pity.

"I really had no idea, Roux, that you were so involved."

"Zach just fucking tell me!" I spat.

I had no idea how Zach was involved in this anymore but

there was one thing that I was certain of. I was sick of being tied up like a dog. My muscles had grown so stiff that I could hardly sit, my headache turning into a constant reminder of the pain I was sure to endure in my time here.

"Declan works with criminals, Roux."

Obviously. He was a lawyer!

"A few years ago, I'm not sure how, but he got in a little too deep with our boss, I don't know the details, I just know the rumours. Boss and him, they made a deal. Declan became a friend of sorts. I don't know why, just that he made sure nothing came to light out any of the boys…incidents. In exchange, he created a list. A list of people that we couldn't touch. People that were safe from any form of harm on our side of the bargain-"

"Zach what the fuck are you going on about!" I snapped.

"You're on the list, Roux!" he whispered, throwing his hands up into the air.

"Why?" I ground out.

"I don't know, Roux," he hissed. "I didn't know that you had anything to do with him until I saw you two together on campus!"

Oh my gosh. The alley. It was the only other time that I had been near Declan, ever. He had put me on the list. Why?

"Then you got shot," he continued. "You weren't meant to, I'm pretty sure our guy had no idea who you were when it happened. Declan didn't care. He dropped all of the cases he had been holding for us. Everything was out in the open, our boss got put away and he's not happy," he grumbled, shaking his head. "Declan should have known better. The agreement was technically void when you got shot, but of course our boss wasn't just going to let him get away with it. The deal was already off, I'm guessing that's why they went after you. To get to him."

Fuck. Oh my gosh.

"Get out."

"Roux, I didn't know they were going to do any of this I swear!"

"Get out!"

"Please, Roux, I swear I only got involved to pay my uni bills!"

I didn't acknowledge what he said, choosing to lay back down on the floor, and hoped that sleep took over my exhausted body soon enough.

I could see him look to the door and then back at me.

"I have a plan," he whispered. "Just be ready."

I didn't have time to respond before the door flung open, hitting the cement wall with force. The stocky man pointed at Zach in anger, before he motioned for the door.

"Out!"

Zach scrambled up and out of the room quickly, not sparing a glance back as he left.

The man walked over to me quickly, each step booming loudly in the small space. As he neared I could see the duct tape in his hands and I tried to squirm away, my scream stuck in my throat. His hand came down quickly in my hair however, ripping me into a sitting position as he bit off a piece of duct tape with his teeth. He looked almost bored, as if this was the easy part of his job. I didn't want to think about it.

The strip of tape was placed harshly over my mouth. I wasn't sure why, it wasn't as if I was going to speak, my throat having closed over in panic. My lungs burnt as I realised my nose had become runny from the tears that streamed down my face. I restarted to hand my head back, as the mucus slowly trailed down the back of my throat. I tried not to think about it, as I held back my gags.

A flash and click had my eyes finding a phone in his hands, pointed at me as if he had just taken a photo.

"Time to see if Marcelo wishes to talk," he grumbled. Standing quickly and walking to the door as he left me sitting against the wall, the tape still over my mouth.

CHAPTER 35

I had no idea how many days I had been here. Zach never came back. It had to have been at least a week. I had been brought water twice, each time the bottle seemed to last me mere minutes before it was empty and my body was screaming out for more. I wasn't sure what they were waiting for, why they hadn't just killed me yet. Clearly Declan wasn't coming.

I found myself thinking, that if I ever got out of this place, I wanted to go back to my hometown. I wanted to go back to my small town, where nothing happened, where I could get a job at the local high school teaching English and never have to worry about any of this ever again. I would be finishing my degree in a few months…pending on how behind I was, then I would be able to do it. I could study from home though, for the time being and move back with my mother.

I could get a coffee from the local coffee shop every day, I could walk the familiar path to work. Most importability, I could forget all about this city and everyone in it. I would make sure my name was never mentioned by anyone here again, never put on another list. In fact, changing my name felt like an amazing thing to do. Something simple, unnoticeable.

I would ask Quinn to come too. She would surely leap at the opportunity to spend time with my mother.

The cell door cut me from my thought, its familiar groan had me forcing myself to sit up. The man who had been in multiple times before walked over casually, reaching down and gripping my face in one hand, whilst the other came to rip off the duct tape over my lips. A breathless cry fell from my mouth at the pain as he tore it off, it felt as though he had taken half my lips with it.

"Up," he commanded.

I tried to find the strength in me to lift my frail body as I gripped the wall, however my legs crumbled halfway, causing me to fall in a heap on the floor.

"Get up. Or I'm going to give you a reason not to stand."

I didn't bother waiting for him to go through with his threat. I already knew that he would. I winced as I dug my nails on the wall, pulling myself steadily until I was wobbling on both legs.

"Good."

My cheek exploded as his harsh slap landed upon it. The breath was knocked out of me as I made contact with the floor and I struggled to draw a breath. The familiar darkness tried to pull me under, however, he didn't allow it. His hands gripped my shirt as he lifted me up from the ground, sneering at me as he shook his head. I didn't mind, I couldn't feel anything. His fist raised and I tried to brace myself. Then, the hallway was filled with commotion. Screaming, gunshots, cries for help sounded loudly through the open door. I was thrown backwards quickly, tossed aside as the man made his way quickly outside, drawing the gun from his pants.

I tried to cough, to breath but nothing worked as my eyes burnt with the familiar tears.

I was ripped from the ground once again, however, Zach's frantic face met mine as he was screaming something I couldn't make out. The ringing in my ears dulled as the dizziness faded in my head.

"We have to go!"

He didn't waste anymore time, throwing me up in his arms and running out of the cell. Pain ripped through me as I bounced around, a strangled scream falling from my lips.

"I'm sorry," he whispered, running us down hallways as he turned and weaved as if we were in a maze.

The noises around us continued to shake the walls and I had no idea what was going on, just that Zach was helping me and we were going to escape.

"I'm so sorry, Roux," Zach breathed as he looked down at me in his arms. "I'm gonna get you out of here."

I felt my body trying to pull me out of consciousness as the walls swirled together. I wouldn't let it though. I was getting out of here! I was leaving! I could see my mum again. See Quinn. I could go and move back home and not worry about any of this. Zach's legs propelled us faster as he ran up a narrow staircase.

"Thank you-"

I was cut off by a loud bang, before something flung us backwards hard. Zach's body tumbled against mine harshly down the staircase as pain ripped through my body. My head hit against the last step with enough force to send my vision black for a few seconds. When I zoned back in, the familiar man from the cell stood at the top of the staircase, a gun in hand pointed directly at us as he slowly started walking down. I gripped Zach rough, trying to get him to move so that we could make a run for it. He remained where he was however and I spun to scream at him to run. Only to come face to face with his open mouth and lifeless eyes as blood dripped from his lips.

A scream tore through my lips as I realised he had been shot.

"Zach!"

The man reached forward and I had no choice but to scramble away and leave Zach, turning back the way we had come. I felt his tight grip on my hair before I could stop my movements and I was flung off my feet, a scream ripping through the air. No! No! I wouldn't go back in that cell!

Sobs wracked my body as I kicked and screamed, trying to scratch, hit, slap anything that I could get my hands on. He snarled, and I found myself bracing for impact.

My body was thrown forward and I caught myself before I hit the ground. I flung myself up quickly as I tried to run. A painful groan had me looking back as I saw him on the ground, hand holding his shoulder which was bleeding onto the floor. Declan stood above him, shaking as he sneered down at him, the gun raised. He looked wild. My breath caught at the sight of him. No. This was his fault! My feet wasted no time in taking off in a random direction. Anywhere to get away from him.

Gunshots could be heard in every direction. Each hallway looking the same as I flung myself around the corners. I screamed as hands gripped at my waist. One came to rest on my mouth as I felt a breath on my cheek.

"It's me," he whispered. I know, I wanted to scream. That's the problem. I found myself crying harder at his words. It was him, the man who had betrayed my trust and put me in this situation.

Screaming, I thrashed against his arms, his hold keeping me tightly against my chest.

"It's okay, no one's going to hurt you!"

As another gunshot rang out from just around the corner however, I found my shaking body giving in. The world grew dark as Derek came into view. The feeling of panic invading me again before everything blacked out.

CHAPTER 36

*E*verything hurt. The burst of pain that shot through my body had my eyes snapping open. White. That was the first thing I saw. The second, was Declan's piercing green eyes pouring into mine with what looked to be unleashed tears. It all hit me like a truck, the memories snapping into place like a broken bone as everything huddled into order. *Oh my gosh. Zach. Zach was, oh my gosh.* A sob escaped my mouth at the realisation, tears brimming in my eyes.

I looked at him with as much hatred as I could muster.

"What?" I tried to snap, however, I found myself struggling to form a sound, my throat closing.

"Please," he whispered. "I just want to explain."

I watched him in anger, trying to form the words to tell him to go away. To explain to him that I wanted him to leave and never come back.

His voice broke as he spoke.

"A year before you found me in the alleyway, I decided that I could use my position to help Derek bring down the criminal activity in the city," he gulped. "I figured if I got close enough with my clients, had them trusting me, that I could funnel the information to Derek."

I couldn't look at him, as I snapped my watering eyes shut. That was so wrong. So freaking wrong.

"I know it sounds bad," he whispered. "But when I found out what they had done, how many people they had hurt, I knew I couldn't just stand by and help them avoid punishment. So, when I was assigned to a high-end drug dealer, I figured if I helped him avoid the charges, I could start gaining his trust. It worked. I told him I wanted in, that I was willing to be their personal lawyer, so that I could gain information and pass it on."

I wanted to scream at him that I didn't care about any of this. That I wanted to know how I came into this whole situation, however, a jumbled slur of croaks fell from my mouth. Declan quickly picked up the picture on the table, pouring me a glass of water and holding it outdoors. I snatched it away quickly, scowling I chugged it down my burning throat.

"One of the dealers in the ring, they caught on to what was happening and baited me to meet them for a deal. That was when he shot me. The morning that you saved me."

His words made my stomach churn. I should have left him there in that alley.

"I knew what Victor, the boss, would do if he ever found out. So the second I woke up, I made sure that Derek had enough information to put him away. Then I realised he may have seen you, that if the dealer in the alley managed to get out or contact anyone, you would be in danger. When we first agreed to work together, I made it clear that there were people who could be brought into this, that if anything were to happen they had to be untouchable. Victor created a list of people that were considered safe. So I put you on it, after I asked Derek for your name from the statement you had to give."

The tears streamed silently down my face as I looked anywhere but him.

"So as long as I worked for them and the dealer stayed in jail, you were safe, so was Derek," his voice broke as he shook his head, seeming angry. "Then you just had to walk past the one fucking deal that I let West go and bust on your campus. The dealer obviously didn't recognise you. You just had to walk past them, pretend you didn't see anything and keep walking!" A tear broke free, running down his face as he shook. "When you were shot, all agreements were off. You had been harmed and therefore I no longer had to keep their secrets quiet. I was angry, so fucking angry. It was never meant to happen! So I told Derek everything. I gave up all cases. Victor was in jail by the end of the week. I was so stupid. I knew I hadn't thought it through but I never thought..." he sighed. "He wouldn't be able to get out, I was sure of that. But he could contact the others and your face had been plastered all over the news. Then they knew who you were, that university campus you were on. I knew they would go after you, so I changed your dorm room, made sure it was on the other side campus. It wasn't enough. So I brought you to my lake house."

"Your office?" I croaked.

"I've been keeping tabs on you ever since I had to put you on that list. I needed to make sure that you were safe. But then you got shot. I had no choice but to ask for Derek's help. I needed to figure out who broke into your old dorm room, who was tracking you down. You were never meant to have to find out about any of it."

I gripped the sheets of the hospital bed in disgust.

"So," I whispered. "I was just some girl that got tangled in your mess and you had to stick around to clean it up."

"No!" he rushed, grabbing my hand quickly.

Pain shot out through my arm at the contact, ripping

through my muscles like a knife, as a whimper fell from my lips.

"Yes, you started out as someone that I just had to take care of but after I met you that day in the hospital, I couldn't help but want to get to know you. I never lied about my feelings for you. I want you Roux."

"Well I don't want you!" I spat. "Get out!"

"But-"

"Get out!" I screamed, ripping my hand from his grip. "You're crazy! I don't want you anywhere near me! Get out!"

His face turned into a defeated frown as he slowly stood from his chair.

"I can leave, Roux, but I'm staying at the hospital."

"No! I want you out of my life," I whispered. "Just leave."

"I need to stay, Derek was shot when we were retrieving you, he's still in the ICU."

I don't feel any resemblance of remorse at his words, throwing him a hard glare as I uttered the words once more.

"Get. Out."

His shoulders slumped, head hanging low as he slowly made his way to the door.

"I'm sorry," he whispered, before disappearing around the corner. As soon as he was gone it was like a weight had been pressed harshly against my ribcage, my breathing becoming shallow as my mind reeled with everything that had happened. Tears spilled over my face as my chest ached. *Why me?* I couldn't help but think. *Why on earth did this have to happen to me?*

My tears turned to sobs which turned to hysteria in a matter of moments. *What was I going to do? How was I going to deal with this?* Everything was messed up. Everything led back to Declan. I couldn't breathe, my chest tightening as I tried to draw in a breath, my eyes burning as I felt the urge to vomit rise in my throat.

"Roux?"

That voice. Frantically, I looked up to meet his familiar brown eyes. His face contorting into a grimace as he took me in, unable to breath and shaking on the hospital bed. What was he doing here? How did he find out about it?

"Mike?"

"I'm here to help," he said softly, walking cautiously to my side as I cried.

As I peered into the eyes of the man I hadn't seen in years, I felt my walls crumbling, one by one and I knew that my whole world was about to come crashing down on top of me. Deja vu ripped through me like a blunt sword, his warm arms pulling me into a tight embrace as I cried harshly into his chest. I had no idea what was going on, but all I could think was, at least he wasn't Declan.

~The End~

TO MY WONDERFUL READERS

I would like to say thank you to the wonderful readers who decided to give this book a chance. Without all your support I would have never been able to accomplish as much as I have. If you enjoyed this book, I would very much appreciate if you could take the time to leave a review, as it would mean so much! I look forward to exploring this wonderful world further with you all in the future.
   -Ayrleah Tull

CPSIA information can be obtained
at www.ICGtesting.com
Printed in the USA
LVHW031254221220
674885LV00006B/302